GRAVE SHIFT

ISBN: 978-1-940222-84-4
First Edition
Printed in the USA

Cover and interior design by Kelsey Rice

GRAVE SHIFT

A DARCY & FLORA COZY MYSTERY

BLANCHE DAY MANOS
& BARBARA BURGESS

𝓟

Pen-L Publishing
Fayetteville, AR
Pen-L.com

Dedications

FROM BLANCHE DAY MANOS: I dedicate Grave Shift to my son Matt Manos and his wonderful family, as well as to the memory of my mother, Susie Latty Day.

FROM BARBARA BURGESS: I dedicate my efforts in this story to my grandson, Max Burgess, who already shows a creative ability and capacity for leadership that would have made his Cherokee and Hispanic ancestors proud.

CHAPTER 1

The letter came on a warm morning in November. Several weeks later I asked my mother if she had a premonition, a tingling in her fingers before she read it. She said no, not even a chill down her spine. However, sometimes it's the everyday events that hold the potential for disaster. Who would have thought that the contents of an innocent looking envelope could turn our lives upside down?

The blank screen of my computer stared accusingly at me. Several national newspapers had picked up my story on *The Changing Face of Rural America* and I was trying to work on two more features, but it was hard to stay indoors on such a beautiful day as this.

Downstairs in the kitchen, my mother made plans for the new school she was building on the Ben Ventris farm south of town. *Ben's Boys*, she was going to call it; a school for boys who needed a home and firm, loving guidance.

No one was more shocked than my mother when Ben Ventris, an old friend of the family, was murdered last spring and bequeathed his farm and all his earthly holdings to her, Flora Tucker.

When she recovered from that unexpected windfall, she started making plans. "This farm would be a wonderful place for boys," she said. "There's that orchard behind the house. There's the river for swimming and fishing, and plenty of trees so the little fellas could learn to chop wood for the fireplace."

Those "little fellows" would actually be juvenile delinquents or boys in danger of going astray from the law. I doubted that they would equate wood chopping with fishing and swimming, but I knew what she meant.

Ben's estate included not only the farm but also his and his daughter's extensive land holdings and another treasure that neither she nor I mentioned. Its location was far too sad to think about. Not many people knew about that hidden vault and that was fine with both of us.

Snatches of the old hymn, *Build Me a Cabin in the Corner of Glory Land,* floated up the stairs as Mom planned how many bunk beds and how large a dining table those boys would need.

Knowing very well what she was doing, I called down the stairs, "Say, Mom, are you drawing up plans for your new house?"

"Darcy Campbell, this house suits me fine. Why would I need a new one? I've got lots of memories of your father within these rooms."

This was an on-going, good-natured battle between us. The truth was, this hundred-year-old farmhouse needed constant repairs. She could afford a new house now and deserved one; preferably one with no stairs to climb or possibly tumble down.

Cliff Anderson, our mailman, came chugging down our road in his old blue truck. We seldom got more than utility bills, bank statements, and sales ads from Williams IGA but Mom looked forward to her daily trip to the mailbox. Most of the friends and relatives who might have written lived here in Ventris County. My mother had been Granny Grace's only child and Dad's parents died a long time ago but I had several cousins and, as Granny used to say, shirttail kin. As far as communicating by email went, Mom refused. The phone and personal chats were her means of communication.

My bedroom window provided an excellent view of the front yard. Mom pulled four items out of the mailbox. Three, obviously too big to be letters from distant relatives in Georgia were probably fliers advertising a seasonal clearance at a store in nearby Tahlequah. As she turned from the mailbox, Mom halted in mid-stride and studied the fourth envelope, a square one. She shook her head then hurried on toward the porch.

Her voice held a note of excitement as she came up the stairs calling, "Darcy, I got a letter from somebody I don't even know in Amarillo."

She tore open the envelope and pulled out two handwritten pages, unfolded them and began reading.

"Who in the world?" she muttered.

"What?" I asked.

She finished the first page and handed it to me. The message was written on plain, lined notebook paper in blunt, no-nonsense cursive:

Dear Flora Tucker: I read about you and your daughter solving the mystery of the murders in Levi after the police were unable to make any progress. I also have a mystery—one that breaks my heart—and I hope you will consider helping me to find a way out of the pain that has engulfed me for more than two years. My name is Sophie Williams. Although you don't know me, I'm sure you will recognize my daughter's name. It was Andrea Worth.

That jerked my eyes from the letter. "Holy cow!! She's the one who . . . ."

Mom nodded, her gaze glued to the second page.

Sophie Williams was right; my mother would recognize the name of Andrea Mott Worth, as would nearly everyone in our little town of Levi, Oklahoma; as well as many people across the country. Although I lived in Dallas at the time, instant recall came to me. Local newspapers had covered the strange series of mysterious events surrounding this young woman.

Less than three years ago, Gary Worth, a wealthy rancher who owned several hundred acres of good pastureland in Ventris County, quietly married Andrea Mott, a 32-year-old divorcee from Amarillo. After only a few months, Andrea Mott Worth disappeared and no one knew where.

"Wait, Mom. I kept that clipping." I jumped up and rummaged through my desk. *The Dallas Morning News,* where I used to work, ran a series of articles on the disappearance. I had cut them out because they concerned my hometown.

My mother silently continued reading Sophie's letter while I re-read the clippings.

According to her husband, Andrea was still in bed when he left at 7 a.m. that September morning. When he came home shortly after noon, she was gone. All of her clothes and personal possessions were in the couple's bedroom. Her handbag sat in its usual place on the dresser, he said. Her red Mustang still crouched in their three-car garage. A housekeeper had been at the Worth home earlier but she reported that she had not seen Andrea at all.

In fact, nobody had seen Andrea Worth since about 6 p.m. the previous day when a landscaper came to deliver an estimate for some tree trimming. He reported that Andrea was the only person at home when he arrived. He gave her the estimate and she promised to call him later. That call never came.

How could she have just disappeared with no trace?

The account of that disappearance brought to mind the disturbing questions asked but never answered. Gary told the police that he was not alarmed when he came home and discovered his wife gone since sometimes a friend picked her up for lunch. By 5 o'clock, he began to worry. He called Andrea's friends and when he got no answers from them, he notified the Ventris County sheriff. No evidence ever turned up, although the couple's vehicles, home, surrounding area, and Gary's place of business underwent repeated testing.

Sunlight gilded the leaves of the oak by the front gate and a chill wind fanned my bedroom curtain. Andrea Mott Worth, young and undoubtedly full of hopes and dreams for the future, had disappeared even more completely than those leaves blowing off the tree and going who knew where.

One of my editors at *The Dallas Morning News* remarked at the time, "I bet that little ole gal just found herself another man and walked off."

Could be. There was certainly no body and no evidence that a murder or kidnapping had taken place.

Mom held out Sophie's second page to me. *Although I am not a wealthy woman,* Sophie wrote, *I do have a little money in savings and would be happy to pay you and your daughter for whatever help you can give me. Please consider looking into my beloved daughter's disappearance. I felt like the newspaper story about your solving the Ventris case was the answer to my prayers and the last hope I've got.*

Sophie's home phone and cell phone numbers followed.

"Well, Mom, what do you think of that?"

She headed toward the stairs. "What I think is I'm going to make a fresh pot of coffee."

A cup of coffee and a talk with my mother solved many a problem during my high school and college years. Strangely enough, today we sipped the dark brew, busy with our own thoughts. Mom's rose bush swaying in the breeze just outside the kitchen window caught my attention.

"It'll soon be nipped by frost," I said.

"What? What'll soon be nipped?"

"Your rose. I was just thinking, Mom, that another season is here and this will be the second autumn that Sophie has faced without knowing the whereabouts of her daughter. How awful that must be for her."

"I agree," Mom said slowly, "and if there's anything we can do to help that poor woman, we ought to do it. With your newspaper connections and the way you can get all kinds of stuff on that computer, and considering that we know just about everybody around here, we might be able . . . you do have a little spare time, don't you?"

Her eyes grew misty and she reached across the table for my hand. "I know just how I'd feel if I was in Sophie's shoes. She must be heartbroken."

I squeezed her hand, realizing again that coming home after Jake died had been the right thing to do. I needed to heal from the loss of my husband and Mom needed companionship. She seemed to be lonelier now than she had been when Dad died twenty years ago. We two women needed each other. And now another woman needed both of us.

"Well, sure, if that's what you want us to do, we could give it a try and see what we can stir up."

A roguish smile quirked my mother's lips. "I kind of like the sound of it. We could even hang a sign out by the mailbox."

"A sign? I don't understand."

"Sure you do. We could hang a sign out there so everybody could see it from the road. A sign that says TUCKER AND CAMPBELL, Private Investigators.

CHAPTER 2

Something warm rubbed my chin; something with a motor. I groaned, rolled over in bed, and opened one eye to see our adopted cat Jethro's close-up unblinking stare. "It's so nice to have a furry alarm clock," I told him. "But you need to be reset to a later hour, Cat. Off the pillow, now. Scoot."

The aroma of fresh coffee wafted up the stairs. Mom always arose before dawn and sat down with coffee and her Bible to start the day. Maybe a cup of caffeine would jumpstart my brain. Sophie Williams' letter plagued my dreams last night. What I knew about Andrea's disappearance kept running through my mind, like a broken record. How was I supposed to come up with information that law enforcement hadn't found? Googling her name on the computer might possibly yield some results, although surely that had been done.

When I came back to Levi after Jake's death, it was with dreams of gardening, writing, and long fishing trips on the Ventris River.

"After our narrow escape this spring, if I get involved in another police matter, I should have my head examined," I told Jethro. He squeezed his eyes together as he contemplated an answer. It took a long time to recover from being in the middle of those violent occurrences. My mother and I had been squarely in the sights of evil that walked around disguised as men. I still couldn't think about my car plunging down Deertrack Hill, the flight through a dark and dangerous tunnel, and coming face to face with a loaded pistol without breaking out in a cold sweat.

Leaving the hustle and bustle of Dallas for the beautiful, hilly scenery of northeastern Oklahoma should have led to a life of peace and quiet, but the sleepy countryside of Ventris County was deceptive and covered dark secrets that were anything but peaceful.

A new idea sprang from lunch at Dilly's Cafe last week with my friend Amy Miller. Right in the middle of dessert Amy asked, "Why don't you write a book about Ventris County, Darcy?"

I almost choked on a bite of strawberry shortcake. "A book? What sort of book and why?"

Amy stopped folding her paper napkin into triangles. "Why not? With your newspaper experience and all the strange happenings around here, you could spin quite a tale. The story of the hidden Cherokee gold is a book in itself. And there are animal legends—I've heard that there may still be panthers in the thickest part of the woods. A few years ago, three of my cousins said a panther dropped out of a tree onto one of the horses they were riding. And, of course everybody has heard about those spooky ghost lights along the river."

"I've personally never come face to face with a panther. And ghost light? The only lights I've seen along the river are from boaters."

She shrugged. "But there have been reports. You might interview people who saw them. You told me Jake left you insurance money. You wouldn't have to worry about income for a while and writing would take your mind off the things you can't help."

By "the things you can't help," she meant my grief at losing Jake. An intriguing idea, to write a book—but about what? A history of the area? A mystery? A romance? Why did Grant Hendley's handsome face come to mind when I thought of romance? I suspected our sheriff could re-ignite those fires of passion we had shared many years ago if I allowed it. The thing was, I didn't want to become romantically involved with anyone. Well, maybe "entangled" would be a better word. Perhaps someday I would feel whole again but I didn't want that empty space in my heart filled just yet.

However, it was definitely a mystery to me that trouble seemed to follow me like a swarm of gnats on a hot summer day. Of course, there were human stories besides those of Ben Ventris. If I wrote a book, should I include a chapter on Andrea Worth? Right now she was an unsolved mystery.

Nothing about Andrea's case made sense. In today's electronic society, people don't just disappear without a trace. But that's what seemed to have happened to her. A few months ago, a small video company in Oklahoma City made a documentary entitled *Into Thin Air* that was picked up by all the major networks. It was about several unsolved missing persons cases, including Andrea's.

Was she murdered? If she was, it was surely efficient because murder always leaves a clue. The state police went over the Worth home, the surrounding grounds, and the couple's vehicles with some of the most sophisticated equipment available anywhere, and not a shred of evidence pointing to violence could be found. None of the neighbors saw or heard anything out of the ordinary. The security guard at the Worth ranch noted only the housekeeper entered the grounds that morning, and the surveillance camera backed up his report. No ransom note appeared. If Andrea was murdered, who murdered her and why? And if it was a murder, what happened to the body? My twenty years as a news reporter had taught me that it was nearly impossible to completely get rid of a human body. But then again, many murders went unsolved for years, possibly even forever.

Besides an extensive ranch, Gary owned a contracting company. Several signs around town proclaimed that the Worth Company had built this or that building. Investigators with dogs covered every single recent construction spot and turned up nothing. Any reporter who has spent a little time in a criminal case courtroom knows the prosecution has to prove that a defendant had means, motive, and opportunity to commit the crime—something that can occasionally be accomplished even if there is no body. But there was nothing to point even a small sliver of suspicion in any direction. There was no body, no evidence, and as far as anybody could tell, no motive of any kind.

In the face of all this non-evidence, what good would it do to go back two years and dig for more information? Did I think I could do a more thorough job than professional crime fighters?

Barefoot, I padded to my closet and pulled out a pair of white walking shorts. After getting dressed, I would crank up the computer. Maybe I could use some of the search engines to discover a clue; some trail, however dim, that I could follow.

My lead investigator had other ideas. Mom stuck her head in the door just as I was tying my white sneakers. She wore a denim skirt and blue shirt. This was her "I mean business" uniform. She had fluffed her black and gray hair around her face, making it look deceptively like a halo. Her sharp glance took in Jethro lying on my unmade bed.

"Get a move on, Darcy. We need to go over to Dilly's for breakfast."

"Sure, if you want to go out for breakfast, that's okay with me. But, I thought it might be a good idea to start on the Worth case."

"We are going to do just that," she pronounced, "and the most logical starting point is the place where everybody in the county comes to drink fresh-ground coffee and eat waffles that Artie's been up making since before daylight. Probably folks around here know a lot more about Andrea Worth than you could ever find out on your computer. And I intend to encourage a little gossip."

"But Mom," I argued, "I'm not comfortable going over there and pumping those unsuspecting people about something that happened a while back."

Wriggling into a Sooners sweatshirt, I presented my case. "I mean, what reason are we going to give for asking such questions? I'm technically on a leave of absence from the newspaper and I don't want anybody to think something else has turned up about Andrea and I'm covering a new story on her."

She tilted her head. "I thought about that. You said that Amy suggested you write a book about Ventris County. You could say that we are interviewing people about that book. And, then sort of sneak in some questions about Andrea, too. You can't tell, Darcy. Somebody might have remembered something that they didn't think was important two years ago. And then again, maybe someone wants to clear their conscience of something they have kept secret. I'm certainly ready to listen to any confessions." She nodded and winked. "I know how to be discreet."

My mom, the psychoanalyst. I ran some coral lipstick across my mouth and brushed my hair into a ponytail. When I turned sixty-seven, I hoped I would look as good as my mother. I inherited her black hair and dark eyes. If only I could acquire her energy and enthusiasm. Glancing in the mirror told me that I looked as good as short notice would allow. Nobody dared fool around with last minute details when Flora Tucker shifted into high gear.

We pulled into Dilly's establishment fifteen minutes later. "We're lucky to find place to park," I muttered. "Where did all these people come from?"

I'm not sure whether Dilly's crowd was due to the Ventris County social hour or the big yellow $3.49 *Breakfast Special* sign in the window. At any rate, I could not see even one empty booth or table as we entered Dilly's. Artie himself waved us toward the end of the counter nearest the kitchen.

"Come on in, Miss Flora and Darcy," he said, grinning. "There's a booth here at the back that is kind of hidden. I'll bet there's room for two skinny little ladies like you."

A sense of hominess settled on me as it always did when I went to Dilly's. This cafe had its beginning way back in Levi history. It opened originally in 1946, started by a returning WWII soldier who loved to cook and loved to eat and decided he wanted to go into business for himself. Because he used fresh vegetables and meat purchased from local farmers, and taste-tested every dish that came out of his kitchen, Dilly's was an instant success. The original yellow Formica and chrome tables and black-and-white checked tile floor had been replaced, but each renovation was done with specially ordered factory merchandise made to replicate the eatery of the forties. Everything was exactly the same—except breakfast was no longer forty-nine cents.

The people who clustered in booths and at the counter didn't allow the joys of eating to hinder the serious business of talking. The restaurant's customers wouldn't have noticed if one of Oklahoma's infamous twisters churned overhead during breakfast. The hum of voices reminded me of a beehive. Before we got halfway across the room, a number of people yelled at Mom, although many in the café were strangers to me. I recognized Pat Harris, treasurer of Goshen Cemetery and Mom's close friend; Chuck Taylor, an old friend of my father's; and Marylee Stratton, owner of the local Cut & Curl.

"Thanks, Tony," I said to Dilly's waiter as he led us to the booth at the end of the room.

"What'll it be this morning, Darcy?" Tony asked, pencil poised above his order pad.

"Blueberry waffles for both of us, please. Nobody can make them better."

As Tony hurried back to the kitchen, I concentrated on the people around me, all of them intent on munching and talking. They seemed pretty contented to me; nobody looked as if he wanted to clear a guilty conscience.

Crispy brown and steaming, the waffles arrived on a thick blue plate. One mouthwatering bite later, I realized Mom had other things on her mind besides breakfast. Her waffles cooled while she worked the crowd like a politician with Election Day right around the corner.

Stopping at her chair long enough to pick up her coffee cup she leaned toward me and whispered, "Have them box up my waffles, Darcy. We'll take them with us. I'm hearing too much now to take time out to eat. I've got to talk to Loretta Walker."

She headed for a corner booth where a couple I did not recognize was about to leave.

Halfway through my breakfast, Pat Harris slid into the seat across from me. "How exciting, Darcy! Your mother tells me you're going to write a book about Andrea Worth," she said.

So much for Mom's discretion. It probably would do no good to tell Pat that she was mistaken, but I tried.

"Not really, Pat. I'm thinking of a book about Ventris County in general. Of course, I'd probably mention Andrea since her case has never been resolved."

From the way her nose twitched, I didn't think she believed me.

Before the lunch crowd arrived, doubtless everybody in Levi would know Darcy Campbell had once again stuck her oar in and muddied the waters of a story that had been nearly forgotten.

As we drove home, Mom and I shared what we learned at Dilly's.

"I guess that most people think Gary Worth's wife did him wrong. Several people mentioned how neighborly he is," Mom said.

"Looks like it. Hiram Schuster couldn't praise Gary enough for the carpentry work he did out at your school. Chuck Taylor told me that Gary actually gave him a calf after one of Chuck's herd was hit by a car on the highway, and the list goes on."

"And Earlene Crowder—you know, she was housekeeper for the Worths for a while—said she had never heard Gary and Andrea exchange a harsh word. She said that Gary is a kind man."

One diner suggested I talk to Jasper Harris, Pat's backward adult son. What could Jasper tell me? Surely he would not be involved in anything nefarious. Although he was a loner and sometimes wound up making situations worse when he intended to make them better, Jasper couldn't be a danger to anybody.

Mom was about to get out of the car as we stopped in her driveway when she snapped her fingers and settled back into the seat. "I forgot to mention that Earlene said Zack didn't come home last night. She was trying not to worry but not doing a very good job of it."

Earlene and J. Lee Crowder were distant cousins of mine. Mom and Earlene were not close friends but they both were interested in the upkeep of Goshen Cemetery and comparing stories about James Tucker, our long-ago common ancestor. Zack was much younger than I and had been born in Earlene and J. Lee's later years, so he and I had little in common. His parents could be accused of hovering where their only child was concerned.

"How old is Zack now, twenty-five?" I asked. "He probably gets tired of reporting in."

"I guess you're right. He drives a truck and I understand he does cross-country hauls at times. Aren't you getting out, Darcy?"

"No, I'm going to talk to Grant. He wasn't the sheriff when Andrea disappeared, but maybe he has found something new about her during these two years."

CHAPTER 3

Grant's receptionist, Doris Elroy, looked up and smiled as I entered. She punched a buzzer and announced my arrival. "Go on in, Darcy."

When I walked through the door marked "Sheriff," Grant was standing with his hands behind his back staring at the falling maple leaves outside his window. I could tell by the set of his shoulders that he was unhappy about something. His tone was as cold as the near-frost conditions which registered on my car.

"Hello, Darcy."

I spoke to his back. "Hi, Grant. Looks like you're deep into solving the world's problems this morning."

His blue eyes shot sparks when he turned to look at me. His expression was not just cold but was downright furious. "Darcy, tell me that what I just heard about your meddling in the Worth case isn't true."

After stepping all the way into his office, I closed the door behind me and sat down in a straight wood chair facing his desk. Gossip in Levi was faster than any form of technology.

"Not meddling, Grant; gathering information. And am I right in surmising that's the reason you are upset?"

"No, Darcy, upset doesn't even come close to the way I'm feeling right now. Here we are with one of the neatest disappearances in local history. The last sheriff and the OSBI couldn't come up with even the smallest clue about what happened two years ago to Andrea Worth. So the investigation just dwindled away. Most of the people in Ventris County decided she just left old Gary. It became a cold case on state records, and as far as civilians like you are concerned, that's the way it should stay. Why did you go to Dilly's and start nosing around? Are you expecting somebody to walk right up to you and say, 'Yep, I know what happened to Andrea Worth.' It won't work that way, Darcy."

A stack of papers flew off his desk as he smacked it with his open hand. He was really mad!

"I just couldn't believe it!" he continued. "A woman as experienced in crime reporting as you are knows very well what kind of trouble she may get into if she goes out and starts asking questions. What if Andrea didn't just walk out on her husband? What if disappearing was not her idea at all? And, doggone it, Darcy, what if the person responsible for Andrea's disappearance was right there in Dilly's? I've been worrying about you ever since you came to Levi and got involved in finding out who killed poor old Ben Ventris. Maybe you couldn't have helped being in the middle of that but . . . ." He paused and brought his voice down a few decibels. "Now you're deliberately asking for trouble."

My own hackles began to rise. "Do you think I'm stupid enough to purposely put myself in danger? You remember that I am, or at least I used to be, an investigative reporter. We're not always the most popular people on earth. Once, somebody even threatened me."

Palms down on his desk, Grant leaned toward me. His eyes narrowed. "Somebody threatened you? Who and when was that?"

Immediately I wished I had kept my mouth shut. "Um, well, it was a few years ago, in Dallas. I had snapped a picture of a man coming out of a drugstore after a robbery. It was my picture that confirmed he was guilty and sent him to jail."

"What is his name and what, exactly, did he say?"

"I'll never forget his name—Rusty Lang. His exact words were, 'I'll get you for this.'"

Grant shook his head. "That only proves my point. Why are you even interested in Andrea Worth after these two years?"

I tried to keep my voice calm. "I've recently found out something that may shed more light on Andrea's disappearance. Don't you think I've been at this sort of thing long enough to know how to proceed?"

"OK, Darcy Tucker . . . ."

"Campbell."

"OK, Darcy Tucker Campbell, what are you talking about? What did you find out?"

"Sorry. I can't divulge a source and this may not amount to a hill of beans anyway."

He kicked his chair toward him and plopped down in it. "We don't know where Andrea Worth is, but let's just say for argument's sake, there was something criminal. If that's true, snooping around can be dangerous. Did you know, Darcy, that here in Levi the drug problem is getting to be pretty bad? Maybe somehow Andrea was mixed up in drugs. You don't want to get in the middle of something like that."

With the desk between us, we sat glaring at each other. Of course I realized that drugs were a problem everywhere, even in small town Levi, but it was sad that it was getting worse. There seemed to be no stopping the trafficking of drugs by unscrupulous people. And the abundance of the gullible who decided to try it just once amazed me. However, "just once" was never often enough.

"*Pinocchio*," I muttered.

Grant looked at me like maybe I had lost my mind.

"The children's story. Many times children's literature holds lessons for grown-ups. In *Pinocchio*, boys who wanted only to go to Pleasure Island were gradually being turned into donkeys and didn't realize it until they were hooked; I mean, it was too late."

His frown deepened. "Yep, that would apply to drugs. But getting back to you—last spring, mostly through sheer luck, you and your mother managed to avoid ending up like Ben Ventris in Goshen Cemetery. I spent several weeks worrying and trying to get you out of harm's way but would you listen? No! Not Miss Darcy, the renowned criminal writer."

So maybe my idea of going through the sheriff's files about Andrea wouldn't work. Grant sounded anything but cooperative.

He picked up a pencil and tapped the eraser end on his desk blotter. "Andrea's case was thoroughly investigated two years ago. That was when Art Grover was sheriff. He called in Steve Hopper from the OSBI. They came up with nothing. Zilch. In fact, Hopper is over in Tahlequah today about a different case. So, Darcy, I don't know what you can hope to uncover."

"I know Steve," I said. "I consulted him a few times in Dallas. Is he at the Cherokee County Courthouse?"

"Don't get any ideas, Darcy. He probably has already gone back to the city. I don't want you and Miss Flora meddling in the Andrea Worth mystery."

Steve! Of course. How convenient that he was nearby. He had the enviable ability to file things away in his memory bank for years.

"We didn't ask to be involved in the Ben Ventris murder last spring, Grant. We just couldn't seem to *not* be involved. It all turned out all right in the end, you'll have to admit."

He reached across the desk and laid his hand over mine. "If you won't consider your own safety, think of your mother. She could be in danger, too. For her sake and my own peace of mind, I sure do hope that you don't start up your own investigation. Surely you know how I feel about you, Darcy, and how I've felt about you since you were sixteen years old. Just drop this crazy idea."

My heart seemed to be choking me and I felt my face grow warm. When I was sixteen, Grant was my first boyfriend. He was my date for the prom and he had kissed me beside the peony bush in my parents' front yard. I had been very sure that I was in love with tall, handsome Grant Hendley. That was before Jake Campbell came into my life. I didn't want Grant to look at me the way he was. I didn't want to hear what he was saying. A person can't just turn back the clock and take up a relationship where it ended. When Jake died, my heart broke and I had learned how very painful love can be. I didn't want to be that vulnerable again.

Pulling my hand away from his, I said, "I'm sorry, Grant, but this looks like something I'm going to have to do. I've got to find out for sure what happened to Andrea. If she ran off, she's bound to be somewhere. I'm going to try to find her. If she met with foul play, well—maybe at least I can help her mother find some peace." I scooted my chair away from his desk and headed toward the door.

"Yes." His voice was quiet. "And you may even get yourself killed, Darcy Tucker."

CHAPTER 4

Twenty minutes later I was in Tahlequah, the capital of the Cherokee Nation. I drove past the old red brick building on the square that was once the county courthouse but now was property of the Cherokee Nation. I remembered going inside the courthouse a few times with my dad when I was a child. The mysterious odor that clung to the rooms, the slow-turning ceiling fans, the brass spittoons, all were novel to me and I felt a child's awe at the intriguing surroundings.

A bench at the edge of the lawn facing the sidewalk was a gathering place for the Spit and Whittle Club, a group of old-timers who sat and talked about local and national affairs. They solved many a problem, even if the solutions never reached farther than the Courthouse Square. Probably a good many governmental dilemmas could have been settled if legislators had the common sense of these men.

A new courthouse had been built in 1979 and the old building was turned back into the hands of the Cherokee Nation as it had been when in was originally built in 1869. I made a mental note to take the time to visit this historic landmark again soon.

Special Agent Steve Hopper of the Oklahoma State Bureau of Investigation rose from his black leather chair in the "new" courthouse when I stepped into the consultation room. A smile began in his dark brown eyes; eyes that I'm certain never missed a thing in his twenty-some years as the agency's lead investigator. I came to rely on this man's knowledge, experience, and understanding of human nature when I was working on a story that spread from Dallas into Oklahoma. He often brought keen insight into a difficult case.

Steve came around the desk and shook my hand. "Darcy, what a nice interruption."

"Thanks for arranging to see me on such short notice, Steve," I said. "I realize you hadn't meant to spend a lot of time in Tahlequah today and rehashing details of an old case wasn't on your agenda."

"No problem," he replied. "I'm just closing out an episode that required me to be in the courtroom for about thirty minutes, so I've got some extra time."

He motioned me to the chair across from his desk as he sat down. "So, Darcy, I understand you've left the newspaper. I guess that means you're not here in a professional capacity?"

"No, I took a leave of absence from the paper after my husband passed away. I just needed some time to think and maybe set new goals. I've always wanted to write a book and now seems to be a good time to start."

"You mentioned Andrea Worth's disappearance when you called. Will that be the subject of your book?"

"In a way. I had actually planned to include a lot of facts and legends about Ventris County, but Andrea's mother sent my mom a letter the other day asking for our help. This is just between you and me, Steve. There was a lot of publicity about Andrea at the time she disappeared and I think I can find ample material. I haven't spoken to a publisher, but I'm pretty sure I can find a market."

"I'd certainly think so. Has anything new come up?"

"Not really."

He leaned forward, put both elbows on the borrowed desk and tented his fingers. "I'll be happy to help you in any way that I can, but I'm sure you're aware I was never officially involved in the case. Ventris County's sheriff at that time called me and wanted some general information because local law enforcement couldn't uncover a shred of evidence that pointed to a murder, an accidental death, a kidnapping, or even a planned disappearance. He had heard I grew up in Amarillo and was acquainted with Andrea's family. Unfortunately I wasn't much help."

"So you don't actually know Andrea's husband, Gary Worth?"

He shook his head. "Although I'd heard quite a bit about Gary and his business interests, I've never met the man. Mainly, what the sheriff wanted from me was an opinion on whether a woman with Andrea's background would simply get up and walk away, maybe with another man, and not even contact her mother. Of course, my opinion was that she would not. But I really don't have any facts in the case other than what I read in the paper."

Opening my shoulder bag, I found my small notebook. "I'm not looking for hard facts here, Steve, not anything that can be proven. I'm here today because I want to draw upon your years of experience in human behavior and your instinct about how people usually respond in difficult situations. More particularly, if you've ever had a gut feeling, a guess, or a theory about what happened to Andrea Worth."

"That sounds fair. But first, let me get us some coffee. Black all right?"

I nodded.

He stepped out into the hall and returned with two steaming paper cups. Settling back in his chair, he thought for a minute.

"Okay, let's begin with what I know is factual, then I'll give you my guess as to what actually came down before she disappeared."

My pen was ready.

"Let's begin with Tom Mott."

That brought me up short. "Andrea's first husband? You think Tom Mott might have been involved?"

His words were cautious. "I think there are a number of possibilities. But let's start with April of 2001. That's when Andrea was married to Tom Mott. I understand she had been away working and then her grandmother died and left her a good-sized inheritance. Andrea came back home to Amarillo and helped her mother in the antique shop her mother owned. Mott had a small ranch just south of Amarillo. He met Andrea shortly after she arrived and immediately made a grandstand play for her. They got married less than two months after she returned."

He shook his head. "Then it gets sticky. Shortly after their marriage, the couple enlarged Tom's ranch by buying a bigger, adjoining ranch."

"With Andrea's money, I presume."

Hopper shrugged. "Well, he didn't have a big ranch before they were married. By the way, I got all this information from a detective in Amarillo, Lee Davis. I'll give you his number if you want to call him."

Yes, I surely would want to call him.

"Some time later, Tom and Andrea got into a fuss of some kind right in the middle of a large restaurant parking lot. Mott pushed her against the car and she fell and was taken to the emergency room to have her knee stitched up."

"Wow! What a rat!"

"Yes, but she declined to press charges. Andrea filed for divorce in a couple of weeks and moved back in with her mother. She lived with her mom for over a year, I believe."

I pondered the implications of these startling facts as he continued, "And that's all I know that can be proven."

I put down my pen. "So what's your gut telling you about Andrea?"

Once again his reply was cautious. "I think there may be something in the divorce file that would help point us in the right direction, but the judge ordered it closed."

"Isn't it unusual for a judge to close a court file in a divorce? And if it happens, it can be opened with a court order, can't it?"

"It is a little unusual for a divorce file to be closed, but it's sometimes done if there's a lot of property involved or if the order contains information that might be damaging to both parties."

There was a lot here I didn't understand. "But isn't Andrea's disappearance sufficient reason to have the file opened?"

"It might be—if there was anything at all that pointed a finger of suspicion at Tom Mott, but there isn't. Mott was at home all that week of her disappearance. He's clean as a whistle."

"And bank records, I suppose, are all considered confidential."

Hopper nodded. "But that changes when a body is found." He drummed his fingers on the desk. "So we need to figure out where she is. And that, Darcy, is my gut feeling about what happened to Andrea Mott Worth."

So Andrea's story began in the Texas panhandle town of Amarillo and ended in Levi, Oklahoma. I was dialing Lee Davis's phone number as I slid into my Escape.

CHAPTER 5

After my interview with Steve Hopper I hurried home to Levi, anxious to see what modern technology could tell me about Andrea's first husband. I also needed to research two other cases of women who had mysteriously disappeared without a clue. Although my book would focus on Andrea Worth, something may have turned up on the other two missing women that would help in our search for Sophie's daughter.

The only thing to do was to go to Amarillo and start digging. Even if it turned out that Tom Mott wasn't involved in her disappearance, their very short marriage had obviously been vitriolic at times, and the repercussions from that were sure to be rooted in Andrea's hometown. The purchase of an adjoining ranch so soon after their marriage looked suspicious in itself, and even if we couldn't get financial details, there was bound to be folks around town who knew the family and were willing to talk.

Mom was sweeping off the front porch when I turned into the driveway. She always insisted the porch should be as clean as the living room floor.

Putting the broom aside, she walked down the steps. "Well, what did you learn from Grant? Was your trip worthwhile?"

Before I could reply, she continued. "I'm sure you didn't stop for lunch and it's almost three o'clock. Come on in the house. I've made sandwiches."

When we were seated at the kitchen table, I told her about talking with Steve Hopper. Then I asked, "How would you like to go to Amarillo tomorrow?"

I thought she'd be surprised, but my mother quite often was one jump ahead of me.

"I was just thinking last night that we ought to go to Amarillo," she said. "After all, that's where Andrea was married the first time, and where she lived and worked for quite a while. It stands to reason there's stuff there we ought to know if we're going to find out what happened."

"Good. I thought we'd leave early in the morning. I've already called Detective Lee Davis. Steve Hopper said he was the officer who did all the background work there, and Davis can see me at four o'clock tomorrow. Maybe we can spend a couple of nights in Amarillo and do a little sightseeing while we're investigating."

Mom smiled. "I'll bet we can find a little café there, too, just like Dilly's. I'll bet this Davis man can tell us if there's an eating place like that. We can go there for lunch and hear a lot of gossip. Sometimes, Darcy, there's a nugget of truth in gossip if a person listens hard. I'll give Sophie a call and tell her we are coming."

Taking my sandwich and coffee, I went upstairs to crank up my computer. Stories of the missing women stuck in my mind because they were particularly poignant. Through the internet, I could read accounts from several different sources. They were bound to contain facts that were new to me.

After a lot of reading, I found that the two women who disappeared into thin air like Andrea Worth were both in their early thirties. One of them lived in Naples, Florida. She vanished in nearly the same fashion as Andrea. Her husband went to work one morning, leaving his wife in the shower. She never did show up for her job as a dental hygienist, but her handbag was missing and her car was discovered later in the parking lot at a local restaurant. That was in October of 1995. No trace of that poor woman ever surfaced. And I found nothing more than that which was similar to Andrea.

The second woman lived near Fredericksburg, Virginia. She was divorced, with a five-year-old son. She drove the boy six blocks to his kindergarten class, then presumably went to her job in a real estate office. Instead, she apparently dropped off the edge of the earth—until 1999 when her body was uncovered in a shallow grave a few miles from her home. There were no clues, no witnesses, no motive, and no evidence at all. In both cases, the husbands were out of town. Real puzzlers. At least the body of that woman had been found although no one was ever convicted of her murder.

I made notes on both cases, then turned my attention to Tom Mott. There was no information on his early years, except that he was the only son of Douglas and Clara Mott who owned and operated a small ranch near Amarillo. Douglas Mott was also a partner in a small local trucking company. Both Motts were killed when their car was hit by a drunken driver. Tom Mott, of course, inherited quite a bit of property. But that didn't seem sufficient to explain the purchase of the ranch he and Andrea bought shortly after their marriage.

Tom Mott had never been married before he met Andrea, and had always lived on the small ranch with his parents. Perhaps he had some money of his own that he invested wisely. Or perhaps his father was a much shrewder money manager than he appeared to be. I was betting that Lieutenant Davis could fill us in on where Tom's money actually came from.

As I sat puzzling over this information, I heard Mom downstairs talking to someone on the phone, probably Sophie. If nothing came from our involvement in this, at least Mom and Andrea's mother had become friends. They talked back and forth several times by phone.

Turning off my computer, I pulled my small suitcase out of the closet.

CHAPTER 6

"Wake up, sleepyhead! We are coming into Amarillo."

Mom yawned and rubbed her eyes. "Did I go to sleep?"

"Probably a hundred or so miles back."

"I like to get up with the chickens, but 4 a.m. is a bit early, even for me."

"I told Lee Davis that I'd meet him in his office at four this afternoon. That was the only time he had available on such short notice. Amarillo is a long way from Levi so that meant we had to rattle our hocks. Sorry for interrupting your beauty sleep."

Mom laughed. "Rattle our . . . . I guess being out here on the prairie is causing you to talk like a westerner."

"Could be. The air is so clean and light, it's probably going to my head; affecting my brain."

Mom reached behind her for a bottle of water. "Hmm. I'll keep that in mind. I like being able to see for miles and miles. Sure is different than the hills and trees of northeast Oklahoma."

"Flat. Plains, grass, windmills, and several oil wells. Lots of cattle enjoy the grass on these plains. Plenty of room here for ranches. But you're right, Mom, it is very different from Levi."

"It's beautiful in its own way, and I imagine these prairies hold some surprises, once a person is out in them, maybe riding a horse through that grass. Notice those arroyos, Darcy. A horse or a cow could fall into one of those and break a leg. I've heard that after a big rain, some of these dry gulches become flooded creeks. They could be dangerous."

Mom was gazing out the window probably imagining what it might be like to live on the prairie.

"Amarillo is the largest city in the Panhandle of Texas and quite historic. There are lots of interesting sites. One thing that has always fascinated me is the Palo Duro Canyon. I'd like to see it," I said.

"So would I. I've seen pictures of it. We'll have to come back when we have a whole lot more time to stay." She looked down at her map. "Up ahead is where we leave I-40. We want to look for Sixth Avenue. It follows old Route 66."

"Shops along Sixth are trying to retain the flavor of the '40s, '50s, and '60s, I hear. They really are attractive! It's like stepping back in time several decades. Look at those storefronts, Mom. Neat!"

"Yes. Sophie said her shop is right along the street. Can't miss it, she said. She told me that her sign is on the front window, Sophie's."

"Just 'Sophie's'?"

"That's what she said."

Antique shops fascinated me with items that people used long ago and were no longer needed.

"If I owned an antique shop, I would think of a more romantic, picturesque name like Past Presents, Bustles and Bonnets, A Backward Look, Lanterns and Lamplight . . . ."

"Rub Boards and Red Hands, Corsets and . . . here it is, Darcy. Pull in right here."

I eased the Escape into an empty parking space. We got out of the car and stretched. "A long drive. Do you think you're ever going to overcome your phobia about flying, Mom?"

She frowned. "Phobia? It's not a phobia, it's common sense. Just think about it, Darcy; when you're on an airplane, there's nothing under you but air for thousands of feet and you sure can't get out to stretch your legs."

A storefront window reached from ceiling to floor on a shop that kids nowadays would call "retro." "Sophie's" was in gold letters above a spinning wheel, a kerosene lamp, and a rocking chair.

A bell tinkled as we stepped inside a room bright with chandeliers fashioned from wagon wheels. A small, gray-haired woman in a floor-length blue cotton dress rushed to meet us.

Although I had never meet Sophie Williams, this woman acted as if my mother and I were old friends or members of her family. She hugged first Mom and then me.

Her dark eyes glistened with tears. "I know who you are. You don't have to tell me. Oh, Flora, Darcy, I am so glad to see you. How wonderful to meet you in person. Come on in. My office is in back. I'm sure you are thirsty. I have a big pot of coffee and a refrigerator stocked with Cokes."

Sophie turned to a younger woman standing behind the counter who was ringing up a sale on an old-fashioned cash register. She, too, wore a dress straight out of the 19th century, a red print with white ruffles on the long sleeves. These women's fashions certainly added to the aura of stepping into the past.

"Carol, I want you to meet Flora Tucker and Darcy Campbell from Levi, Oklahoma. Carol has been my right hand since Andrea left to marry Gary. Can you please take care of customers for a bit, Carol, while I talk to our visitors?"

The woman smiled. "Sure. Nice to meet you two."

We shook hands with Carol then followed Sophie past butter churns, flatirons, cane-bottomed chairs, coffee grinders, sets of brightly colored dishes, and a bedroom suite complete with canopy bed. She opened a door at the back of the shop and stood aside for us to enter.

Sophie's office was snug and homey. Pale yellow curtains covered a small window. A ledger, telephone, and computer sat on her desk. A framed picture of a smiling young woman was turned so that I got a good look at her before I sat down. Andrea. The resemblance between mother and daughter was striking.

Sophie settled us into two over-stuffed chairs and stood facing us.

"Would you prefer coffee or a Coke?" she asked.

We said "Coffee" in unison.

Sophie laughed. "Nothing like a good cup to restore a person. You both must be tired out. I appreciate your making that long drive. I've been wanting to talk to you in person. You said on the phone last night, Flora, that Darcy is to talk to Lee Davis today. I'm glad. I've talked to him several times, but I think it's best if you hear what he has to say firsthand instead of through me."

We accepted the coffee that Sophie brought us in white china cups with tiny pink roses around the inside, with a thin, gold ring circling the top. The same pattern was repeated in the saucers. An admirer of antiquity, I handled the fragile cup reverently.

"While Darcy is talking with Mr. Davis, I thought I would see about renting a room for the night," Mom said. "Which motel would you recommend, Sophie?"

"Hotel Sophie Williams," she said promptly.

"Oh, no," Mom protested.

"Now listen," Sophie said, "I will feel really hurt if you don't come home with me. I have a big old empty house and several spare bedrooms. There's not a reason in the world for you to go to an impersonal motel."

Refusing this woman really would wound her sense of hospitality. Mom looked at me and nodded.

"We thank you, Sophie," Mom said. "We certainly did not expect you to be burdened with us."

"No burden," Sophie assured us. "I hope you stay long enough to see a few of our Amarillo attractions, and I want you to be sure and go out to look at Andrea's ranch."

"Do you mean the ranch she and Tom Mott bought?" I asked.

Sophie shook her head. "Oh my, no. What I mean is the ranch that Andrea's grandmother left her. It's southeast of town, past the Palo Duro Canyon which, by the way, is worth the trip in itself. This ranch of Andrea's, the Inglenook, is the biggest ranch around; a whole lot bigger than Tom's spread."

This was an unexpected twist. "So the ranch did not belong to both Tom and Andrea? It was only Andrea's?"

Sophie nodded. "Yes. It has been passed down to Williams descendants for four generations. In her will, Andrea's grandmother Williams stipulated that it must never be owned by anyone who wasn't a Williams descendant or the spouse of a descendant. So that's one thing Tom didn't get his hands on. Yet."

A note of bitterness crept into Sophie's voice. I was about to question her further when I heard a loud noise out in the store.

"No! I want to see Aunt Sophie! I definitely will not talk to anyone else!" shouted an unseen female.

Sophie sighed and rose to her feet. "I'm sorry. Sounds like it's my niece, Charlene, again. I'll be back as quickly as I can."

Before Sophie reached the office door, it flew open and a young woman with stand-up spiky blond hair, whose heavily made-up face resembled a thundercloud burst into the small room. She carried a kerosene lamp with a lovely glass shade, half of it broken off.

She thrust the lamp toward Sophie. "Look at my lamp! Your hired help didn't wrap it well and when I got home, I found this. And now the impudent woman won't refund my money. She said I probably dropped it!"

"See if you can find a replacement, Charlene," Sophie said, reaching for the lamp. "If you can't, of course I'll give you your money back. If you'll calm down, I'd like you to meet . . . ."

But Charlene stomped out of the room, slamming the door behind her.

Sophie set the lamp on her desk and ran a hand across her forehead. "I'm sorry. That Texas tornado was my niece . . . actually, my husband's niece, Charlene Williams. Charlene is a story all in herself and I'm afraid it isn't a pleasant one."

"We're listening, if you want to tell us," Mom said quietly.

Sophie sank into her upholstered desk chair.

"It goes way, way back. Charlene is a few years younger than Andrea and she was always jealous of my daughter. I'm not sure why. And her temperament is not the best, I'm afraid. Maybe she is actually a lot like her grandmother. Grandma Williams was a mean-tempered old gal."

I couldn't muffle a giggle.

"Excuse me, but she was. And bullheaded! I have never seen anybody as stubborn as my mother-in-law. Anyway, she stipulated in her will that the Inglenook Ranch was to go to Andrea. That didn't set well with Charlene because there were only the two grandchildren: Andrea and Charlene. She thought Grandma Williams should have divided the ranch, but that piece of Texas has been handed down intact from one Williams to the next for four generations and that's the way it's going to stay."

Sophie's strong coffee was beginning to make me feel human again. I carefully set the empty cup with its saucer on her desk.

"So Charlene didn't much like Andrea?"

"No, she didn't. And I guess she has taken as her mission in life to make me miserable. She wants me to talk to a lawyer about breaking Mom Williams' will. She wants Andrea declared dead, but we can't do that yet. It has been only two years and I keep hoping my daughter is alive—somewhere. Anyway, that little episode with the lamp is an example of one of the ways Charlene keeps needling me. I don't know about that girl." She shook her head. "Sometimes I think her brain is addled."

"I'd like to talk to her," I said. "Do you have her phone number?"

"Yes, I have it," Sophie said. "But you don't have to meet Lee Davis 'til 4:00. Let me take you out to my house and get you settled in my guest room. You can unwind and rest a bit after that long drive

33

CHAPTER 7

Sophie's white frame house, shaded by giant cottonwoods, sat at the end of a long driveway in a quiet neighborhood. Three round columns supported a wrap-around porch. Low-growing herbs, still green, bordered the walk. When Mom and I walked up the steps behind Sophie, I could see why she loved this place. And Andrea—had she loved it, too?

Braided rugs were scattered across the pine floor in a large, sunny room. "Sophie, your house is wonderful," Mom said.

"Thank you. It is where Andrea grew up. My husband and I moved here after we were married and I've lived here ever since."

She showed us to our upstairs room. Bright Texas sunlight streamed in through large windows hung with white crisscross curtains. Handmade quilts covered the twin beds. Suddenly, I realized how tired I was.

We dropped our suitcases on the floor. "This is lovely, Sophie," I said. "We can't thank you enough."

She waved away our gratitude. "I'm honored that you are here. The bathroom is right through that door. Help yourself to whatever is in the refrigerator in the kitchen and just pull the door closed behind you when you leave. It'll lock. I'm going to have to get back to the shop."

"I believe I'll go with you," Mom said to me as Sophie left. "I want to meet this Lee Davis person."

Long before we reached police headquarters, I began to wish that my appointment with Lee Davis had been scheduled for tomorrow. My mind had been in overdrive all night working over the things Steve Hopper told me and I had had very little sleep. Now, even with plenty of coffee, my eyes felt scratchy and I was as alert as a bear disturbed in the middle of hibernation. Which is to say, drowsy.

As it turned out, we needn't have hurried. The receptionist, whose name tag said Tiny Monroe, told us Lieutenant Davis had been called out on an emergency but another officer, Sergeant Maria Romero would meet with us. Ms. Monroe looked us over and nodded, apparently satisfied with what she saw.

She shifted her wad of gum to the back of her mouth and talked around it. "About time somebody from Levi came to talk to us. Although I think it's mighty strange that you're coming after Andrea has been gone for two years. That first husband of hers, that Tom fellow, didn't like being thrown over for another man. Those Motts hold long grudges, let me tell you."

"Thank you, Tiny." A tall, slim woman came from an inner office. She frowned at Ms. Monroe and shook her head. Under her arm she carried a blue, legal-sized folder.

"I'm Maria Romero," she said, extending her hand.

Her honey-colored skin, black hair, and dark eyes spoke clearly of her Hispanic background. She wore her hair pulled back into a bun and her makeup had been applied sparingly. I had the feeling that this woman was truly a professional.

Maria escorted us to her office on the second floor and invited us to sit in the two chairs in front of her desk.

"Actually, Lieutenant Davis did want to meet with you," she said, "but he thought I'd be the next logical choice because I've lived here all my life, been a police officer for fifteen years, and know just about everybody in town. Although I wasn't well acquainted with Andrea

Worth, I do know quite a bit about her family background and I knew her first husband. In fact, I went to high school with Tom Mott."

Mom, never one to mince words, leaned toward her. "If you knew Tom, can you tell us what he was like? Was he outgoing, shy, or what? Did he have a temper? From what we've heard, sounds like he was pretty easily riled."

Maria raised her eyebrows and looked from her folder to Mom. "Pretty fiery, I'd say." She rifled through some papers in her folder. "I understand that, according to Lieutenant Davis, you have already spoken with Steve Hopper? He gave you some of the background on Andrea and Tom Mott's marriage?"

"Yes, he said that Andrea and Tom had a rocky marriage that didn't last long. But Lieutenant Davis told me on the phone last night that Tom was on his ranch at the time Andrea disappeared and couldn't have made the trip to Levi and back without somebody being aware he was gone. His ranch hands and several town folk said they had seen him right here in Amarillo."

"That's true. The investigating officer's notes say the only time the police were called was during a restaurant brawl when Tom got a bit physical. But I happen to know there were at least two other times when a loud argument was overheard right here on a city street."

Sergeant Romero propped her chin in her hands. "You know, I was surprised when I first heard that Andrea had married Tom. He had the reputation of being a real womanizer and someone who did business with a bunch of mighty questionable cohorts. On the other hand, Andrea always seemed to be a hard worker and a smart businesswoman. I heard that she made several changes in her mother's shop that increased sales considerably. I also heard that Andrea's mother didn't even know about the wedding until it was a done deal."

Sophie never told us that.

Mom rubbed her upper lip and squinted at something in the distance, a sure sign she was deep in thought. "Of course, after they were divorced, Andrea re-married. Seems to me if Tom had been inclined to get rid of his wife, it would have been more profitable for him to have done that when he could have inherited a chunk of her money."

Maria nodded. "You would think so. However, I do know that in their divorce settlement, Tom kept the ranch he and Andrea had bought together. And it borders that great big Inglenook Ranch that she inherited from her grandmother."

"OK, I've got to know something. I didn't mention it to Sophie because I didn't want to sound rude—but Inglenook? What kind of name is that?" I asked.

"It's a very pretty name." Mom smiled. "It means a fireside or a chimney corner. Your own Grandma Grace, Darcy, liked to curl up with a book in a corner by the fireplace. It was her favorite reading place, she said, when she was a girl."

Hmm. A person never grows too old to learn something new.

"So, did Andrea inherit a lot of money plus the ranch from her Grandma Williams?" I asked.

"I don't know how much money, but I do know that Eudora Williams was considered a millionaire around town." Again, Ms. Romero consulted the folder. "Of course, it's no secret that the ranch went to Andrea at her grandmother's death. The title to the ranch was transferred to Andrea on the county records. The section of land that Andrea and Tom bought later would be considered joint property, but nobody knows if he got his hands on some of her other money, and nobody has access to her banking records at present. If Andrea's body is eventually discovered, then probate kicks in and that leaves a lot of things open to official scrutiny."

She continued. "I hesitate to even mention the other thing I've wondered about. This is probably only gossip, but it could be important to the case; I don't know. There is a niece, Charlene Williams, who worked for Eudora Williams off and on for several years and she was convinced that her grandmother would divide the Inglenook ranch between her and Andrea. When she learned that Andrea got the whole ranch, several folks heard Charlene say she wouldn't stand for it; she'd take care of Andrea. Of course, that was probably just empty threats from a jealous woman."

Charlene Williams was fast becoming a most interesting character in this tragedy. I would call her as soon as I could.

"But surely, since there were only two grandchildren, Charlene was not left out in the cold by her grandmother; no inheritance at all?" I asked.

Sergeant Romero shook her head. "Charlene got a rental property in town and, I think, some heirlooms. But she really wanted that ranch."

She paused. "I do know that Charlene was at work the day Andrea disappeared."

We thanked Sergeant Romero for her time and headed for the elevator.

"Well," my mother said, "it looks like everybody who might have had a hand in Andrea's disappearance was conveniently occupied elsewhere; that's strange in itself, but it could happen. So maybe she did just up and leave on her own."

Mom had spoken as we walked by the desk belonging to Tiny Monroe.

"And then again, maybe not," Tiny muttered.

I turned around and looked at her. "What did you say?" Tiny shrugged and picked up a sheaf of papers. Turning her back to us, she stalked over to a file cabinet. I looked at Mom. She shook her head.

"I think the interview is over," Mom said.

CHAPTER 8

As it turned out, I did not call Charlene Williams that night. For supper, Mom and I took Sophie out to eat. It seemed little enough that we could do in return for her hospitality. I had never been a big meat eater; in fact, I thought I could happily eat only fruit, nuts, and vegetables the rest of my life, but the steak I had that night at one of Amarillo's most popular restaurants was enough to make me change my mind.

After supper, feeling comfortably full and sleepy, my only thoughts were of that inviting bed in Sophie's upstairs guest room. I must have been asleep by the time my head hit the pillow.

The next morning the aroma of fresh-ground coffee made me think for a moment that I was at home until I realized that Sophie must be an early riser, too. I glanced at the other twin bed—empty. I was sure that my mother and Sophie, these two newfound friends, were downstairs talking.

Quickly slipping into my blue robe and fuzzy slippers, I followed my nose down to the kitchen.

Sure enough, Mom and Sophie were sitting in the small breakfast alcove, sharing cups of coffee and a morning chat. Tears shone in Sophie's eyes and I guessed they had been talking about Andrea.

Mom turned in my direction. "Sophie was just telling me about Andrea's ranch, the Inglenook. She would like for us to see it today. How does that sound to you?"

"Please help yourself to coffee, Darcy," Sophie said. "I hope you like flapjacks. Bacon is there on the stove, too. Everything is still hot."

Pouring coffee into a waiting cup, and snagging some bacon, I followed my hostess's directions. "That sounds great, Mom," I said. "But will you have time to do that, Sophie? What about your shop?"

"I've talked to Carol. She can handle things today. She's very competent. Did you two bring jeans, something that can straddle a horse?"

Mom's eyes grew large. "You want us to ride horses?"

Sophie smiled. "Can you?"

"Well, sure," Mom said. "I guess. Darcy?"

"That sounds like fun. It has been a long time since I've been on the back of a horse."

"It's the best way to see the Inglenook," Sophie said. "Some ranchers have started using ATVs but we prefer the horse. He's much quieter and, in a pinch, can maybe get a cowboy out of trouble. Besides the All-Terrain Vehicle is noisy and scares the cattle. The ranch is out beyond the Palo Duro Canyon. It's a wonderful canyon about twenty-five miles southeast of town."

An hour later we were on the rim of the fabled canyon, the second largest in the United States. I could hardly believe my eyes. It was breathtaking and a complete departure from the flatness of the prairie.

Sophie braked her Ford truck and we tumbled out to stare at this natural wonder.

The only word I could think to say was, "Amazing."

"It's 120 miles long and twenty miles wide in places," Sophie said. "The deepest part is over 800 feet. Beautiful, isn't it?"

"Beautiful" didn't do the canyon justice. The moss greens, yellow ochre, rust, and mauve canyon walls spread out below me as far as I could see. Scudding clouds continually changed the colors.

"What caused all this?" Mom asked. "Of course, I know that God did, but what did He use?"

Sophie laughed. "He used the Prairie Dog Town Fork of the Red River. That and wind have gradually eroded these rocks."

Mom pointed into the distance. "I could swear that's a lighthouse over there."

"In a way, it is," Sophie said. "At least, that's what the rock formation is called."

"Palo Duro. What a place. And what does its name mean?" I asked.

"It's Spanish for 'hard wood,'" Sophie said. "Yes, it's a remarkable area. The deer, wild turkey, coyotes, mountain lions, bobcats, rattlesnakes, and many other animals seem to enjoy it. Of course, it's their natural home, and like us humans, there's no place like home."

"Did you say 'rattlesnakes'?" I climbed back into the truck. "Maybe the best way to view the canyon is from the safety of your truck, Sophie."

"It's time we moved on anyway. The ranch is a few miles farther and I want us to have plenty of time to explore."

Thirty miles later, Sophie turned her truck from the main road onto a narrow graveled lane. A tall iron gate straddled the lane. A wood sign swung from the top of the gate. One word, "Inglenook," had been burned into the sign.

"What's that beside the ranch name?" I asked, pointing at a symbol etched into the sign.

"It's a flame," Sophie said. And of course the W under it is for Williams. The flaming W. It's the ranch's brand."

We bumped across a cattle guard and were within the Inglenook. A long driveway curved around a small pond, bordered by a few willows.

"I'm glad there's plenty of water in the tank," Sophie said, as we bounced past.

"Tank?" I asked.

"The pond," Sophie said, grinning.

Three sorrel horses looked up as we passed. I couldn't see any sign of human habitation until we topped a small rise; there, spread out in front of us were enough buildings to furnish a small town.

"Are all these a part of the ranch?" Mom asked.

"Yes," Sophie said. "It takes a good many buildings to run a 30,000 acre cattle ranch. In addition to the main house, there's the house for the overseer, the bunkhouse for the cowboys, cook shack, tack room, machinery shed, gasoline tanks, the barns; a lot of buildings but each one plays an important part on the ranch."

"My favorite is the big, red old-fashioned barn that looks like it belongs in the 19th century," Mom said.

"Actually, it does. That's the original barn. It has been kept in good repair, re-roofed and painted when needed."

"Always painted red, I'll bet," I said.

"Yes. Old-timers used materials they had on hand: ferrous oxide, milk, linseed oil, and lime. The paint had the added attraction of killing moss and stuff they didn't want growing on the walls. The ferrous oxide caused the paint to be red and we've kept up that color 'cause it seems to fit. Now, let's go over to the horse corral and see what Oscar has picked out for you to ride."

Oscar turned out to be one of the ranch hands. He was standing by a group of horses in the corral, a curry comb in his hand. He looked up as Sophie parked the truck and we three women tumbled out.

He touched his wide-brimmed hat. "Miss Sophie," he said. "These fellas ought to be just about right for you all."

Three horses; two pintos and a shiny black, were saddled and bridled, their reins looped loosely around a corral post.

Sophie's mount was the quarter horse. "Star" she called him because of the white spot in his forehead. The pintos were for Mom and me.

The cook had prepared sack lunches for us and Sophie slipped these into Star's saddlebags before putting her booted foot into the stirrup and swinging onto his tall back. Sophie had brought along two hats that, happily, fit us. She told us we needed them to protect our faces from the sun. I wasn't sure whether the wind would let them stay on our heads, but Sophie was the expert here. Oscar helped Mom into the saddle. I determined to mount on my own so I grabbed the saddle horn, stuck the toe of my left boot into the left stirrup and swung up. Funny how tall I felt on the back of this little pinto. Sophie led the way and our horses, Mint and Julep, obediently trotted after Star as he left the corral.

"How you doing, Mom?" I asked as I glanced over at her.

My mother wore a grin that took about ten years off her face. "I haven't had such a lot of fun in a long time," she said. "I had forgotten how much I used to enjoy riding."

I had to admit, it was exhilarating. I could understand how my ancestors must have loved their horses and the feeling of being in control of all this bridled power. Hopefully, tomorrow my muscles wouldn't be paying for the fun I was having today.

The prairie stretched away from us on all sides. Wind blew the grass in waves reminiscent of the ocean. The denim jacket I wore felt welcome because, although the sun shone, the wind definitely was chilly.

The rise and fall of the landscape was so gradual that I didn't realize we weren't riding through flat land until I looked behind me and could see no sign of the ranch buildings. In the distance, white-faced cattle grazed. The sky shone with a clean blue so bright that it hurt my eyes. There was no sound in all the world except the clop of our horses' hooves, the creak of saddles, and the wind blowing through the sage.

Sophie dropped back to ride between us. "This is where the Inglenook borders the Mott ranch," she said. Drawing back on the reins, she looked down. "What's this?"

A roll of barbed wire with some fence posts stacked beside it lay in our path. Mom and I stopped Mint and Julep beside Star. Sophie slid off her mount and kicked the posts. When Sophie looked up at us, her cheeks were flushed.

"That Tom Mott! He is trying to fence off part of our land again. He did this once before and I had to go talk to a lawyer to prevent him from actually taking part of our land! He wants this ranch so bad that he will stop at nothing to get it. He doesn't care whether it's all in a parcel or little bits at a time, just so he gets the Inglenook!"

Did Sophie realize what she said about Tom stopping at nothing? Maybe my tired brain wasn't functioning full throttle but this was hard to puzzle out. The Inglenook Ranch belonged to Andrea. She had been Tom's wife but divorced him and re-married. After her second marriage, she disappeared. Legally, the ranch was still hers because it was too soon to have Andrea declared dead. But how would it profit

Tom for Andrea to be dead? The ranch was out of his reach anyway, wasn't it?

Sophie frowned as she swung back into the saddle. She pointed to a large, spreading cottonwood standing like a lonely sentinel atop a knoll in the vastness of the prairie. "Oh, let's forget about it for now and not let that miserable Tom Mott spoil a perfectly nice day. There's a spring over there by those trees and some flat rocks. It's a good picnic place. That's where we'll stop for lunch," she said.

This was welcome news. Breakfast happened a long time ago and something about being in the open air gave me an appetite.

I gingerly dismounted and clung to the saddle horn until I was sure I could walk.

Mom laughed. "I think you could be called a tenderfoot, Darcy."

She was already standing with Sophie under the cottonwood, helping spread our lunch on the flat-topped gray rock.

How had she dismounted so quickly and walked with no assistance after that ride? "It's not my feet that are tender," I said. "Aren't you even just a little bit stiff?"

"No more than usual. At my age, I get used to a few aches and pains; not like you youngsters who just haven't been around as long!"

She winked at Sophie and they both giggled like two schoolgirls.

Following Sophie's lead, I tethered Mint to a scrub bush and hobbled over to join them.

"Your cook knows how to put together a meal!" I said as I bit into a roast beef sandwich.

"Yes, I do believe that Myron is probably the best cook in the county."

"Myron? I expected a name like Slim or Cookie or Sourdough."

Mom answered for Sophie. "Good heavens, Darcy, I think all you know about the West is what you've read in books."

Sophie shaded her eyes with her hand and looked into the distance. "Uh-oh," she said. "Here comes trouble."

A horseman topped a ridge and trotted in our direction. Reining in, he rested his arms on the saddle horn and leaned toward us.

Sophie got to her feet and faced him. "Tom Mott, what are you doing out here?"

The man sitting astride his beautiful bay horse seemed to be perfectly at home in the saddle. Looking up, I met a pair of the most hostile hazel eyes I had ever seen. So this was Tom Mott, Andrea's first husband. He wore a dusty black hat over longish sandy hair, a light blue jacket and faded blue jeans. Tom was a small man, wiry and muscular. His lean face was set in hard lines. How could Andrea have been attracted to a man who looked like a picture straight off a wanted poster? Did she enjoy an element of danger? There was just no accounting for whims of the heart.

"I could ask you the same question, Miss Sophie, ma'am."

Sophie's voice was low and tense. "This is my ranch. I have every right to be here."

"Maybe. Maybe not. I'm thinking the surveyor I've hired may have a different idea about this strip of the Inglenook. Did you notice I'm ready to run a fence to be sure that my cattle don't mix with yours? Pretty neighborly of me, I think."

Sophie's hands clenched into fists. Mom and I scrambled up to stand beside her. "You know good and well that your property line is back at least half a mile," she said through clenched teeth. "What no-good surveyor and lawyer have you hired this time?"

Tom Mott looked for all the world like a sly fox when he grinned. "I guess we'll just have to wait and see, won't we, Miss Sophie Ma'am?"

He lifted the reins and his horse moved away at a gallop. We watched until he disappeared below a swell in the prairie.

CHAPTER 9

"Our last night in Amarillo," I said and sighed. We three women huddled under warm afghans, tucked around us in Sophie's wicker rockers on her front porch. The starry sky seemed almost close enough to touch. The lonely cry of a coyote rose and fell on the wind.

"Those stars up there look a lot bigger than they do in Levi," Mom said. "Must be the clear air."

"Higher elevation, too, I imagine," Sophie said. "You don't really have to go back home, you know. You are welcome to stay as long as you like."

"We've accomplished about all we came to do," I said. "I've met and talked with you and Sergeant Romero, and I've met the formidable Tom Mott. Only thing I haven't done is interview your niece Charlene. I dialed her number three times and she doesn't answer. I get the distinct impression she doesn't want to talk to me."

Sophie shook her head. "Could be. I gave you her cell phone number and I'm sure she has the phone with her. Well, you tried, Darcy. That's all anyone can do."

Yes, that was all I could do.

"Did you get any information that you think may be helpful in your search for Andrea?" Sophie asked.

Actually, I didn't know. True, I now had more of a feel for Andrea's life before she married Gary Worth and came to Levi. I had met her first husband. I knew that Tom wanted, above all else, to own all or part of Inglenook. I wondered if that might have been the reason he married Andrea. But Tom had an alibi for the time of Andrea's disappearance, as did her spiteful cousin. Besides, why would Tom kill or kidnap Andrea now? If that had been his plan, surely he would have done so while he was still married to her.

Before I could answer Sophie, a Crossfire Roadster wheeled into Sophie's driveway and parked under the yard light. "Well, well, Darcy. It seems you are about to get your wish," Sophie said.

A young woman slid out of the sporty white car with the black ragtop and came up the walk.

"Good evening, Charlene. Pull up a chair," Sophie said.

"Hi, Aunt Sophie. I'll perch here on the railing. I haven't long to stay," Charlene said.

Sophie motioned toward Mom and me. "Charlene, I wanted to introduce you to my visitors earlier. This is Flora Tucker and Darcy Campbell."

The young woman nodded. Her face was mostly in shadow but I thought she seemed troubled. "I know who they are. Carol, your helper told me."

"Did Carol refund your money for the lamp?"

Charlene shrugged. "Oh, sure. All it took was a word from you. Actually, I came to tell you something, Aunt Sophie. You will hear it anyway and I'd rather you hear it from me so you can be happy for me."

I sensed Sophie's tenseness. Whatever it was Charlene had to say, I had the feeling that it probably would not make her aunt feel terribly jolly.

Charlene slipped off the railing and held her left hand out toward us. A ring with a large diamond glittered in the moonlight.

"A ring? An engagement ring? Why, that's wonderful, Charlene. Who is the lucky man?"

"Tom Mott."

Sophie gasped and I could feel her shock and dismay. Looking up at her niece, she slowly shook her head. "Tom? Oh, no, Charlene."

Charlene jerked her hand away and crammed it into the pocket of her tight Levis. "Why not? Tom loves me and I—well, I've loved Tom for a long time."

Sophie drew a deep breath. Her voice sounded tired as she said, "Oh, Charlene, dear child, I hope you'll reconsider."

Charlene stamped a booted foot. "Look, Aunt Sophie, let's put our cards on the table, shall we? You know that I've always been crazy about Tom. I loved him even before he married Andrea. She took him away from me, and you know she did! But then, I guess she paid for it, didn't she?"

I spoke before I had time to consider my words. "What do you mean, 'she paid for it,' Charlene?"

Charlene backed up. Her voice sank to a whisper. "I don't mean what you're thinking. I would never hurt Andrea. Never. Yes, Granny gave her the ranch and it should have been half mine. That was so unfair! But I am not responsible for her disappearance."

Standing up, I faced Charlene. "But you know who was responsible."

"No. No, of course I don't. Why ever would you think that?"

Her chest rose and fell in quick gasps. Her face looked flushed. Something was troubling this young woman. She had come for more reasons than showing her aunt the diamond ring.

I recalled the receptionist, Tiny Monroe, and her comment as we left Lee Davis's office. Mom had said that it looked like everybody was busy when Andrea had disappeared.

"And then again, maybe not," Tiny had said.

The woman who stood in front of me now was more than excited; she was scared. Had she come to check me out? Maybe she wondered just how much I knew about Andrea. Tiny's words as we left Sergeant Romero's office may have been more than just the empty gossip of a nosy woman. She had insinuated that not all the possible suspects had an alibi at the time of Andrea's disappearance.

This could be the right time for a bluff. I decided to risk it. "You went to Levi. You saw Andrea."

Charlene swallowed. Abruptly sitting down on the porch rail, she grabbed the post for support and stared at me, her eyes wild.

"How—how did you know?"

Crossing my arms over my chest, I said, "I didn't."

Charlene began to cry, her shoulders shaking. Between sobs, the words tumbled out, scarcely audible. "I knew when I heard that you were here in Amarillo that you would keep digging. I've heard about you and your work for the *Dallas Morning News*. I've read some of your stories. I knew you wouldn't let well enough alone. Yes, I did go to Levi and, yes, I did see Andrea!"

Sophie's afghan slid to the floor as she sprang to her feet. She grabbed her niece's arm, as taught as a bow string. "Charlene! Do you know what happened to my daughter?"

Charlene stared at the floor. She covered her face with her hands and tried to control her tears. "I swear to you, Aunt Sophie, I do not know what happened to Andrea. I went to Levi a week before she disappeared. I went to try to talk some sense into her head. I wanted her to sign over half of the Inglenook to me. Tom was so unhappy and I just wanted to make him happy, make him love me like I love him. But Andrea wouldn't listen. She said that I would probably turn that wonderful ranch into a housing development. But I would never have done that. When I left her, Aunt Sophie, I swear to you she was as alive as you or I."

The only sound on the porch was the wind sighing around the corner and Charlene's labored breathing.

Then slowly, Sophie spoke. "I see. Yes, I understand. I believe you."

Charlene wiped her eyes with the back of her hand. Her voice was a whisper. "Thank you, Aunt Sophie. Andrea and I were not friends, but I never would have hurt her. All my life I wanted to be like her. She was Granny's favorite and she took Tom away from me. If only Granny had been fair and left half the ranch to me."

The three of us sat silently as we watched Charlene stumble down the sidewalk, her shoulders sagging. The little car backed out of the driveway and its taillights disappeared into the darkness.

"Yes," Sophie said, "if only Mom Williams had treated the girls equally."

But she hadn't. The shortsightedness and selfishness of adults sometimes cost children dearly. It had done so with Charlene. Like Sophie said, Eudora Williams was a mean old gal.

Envy, greed, revenge; all of these were ingredients that could never have a happy outcome. Something clicked in place for me. If Andrea were dead and if Charlene had the Inglenook and Tom married Charlene, that beautiful ranch would at last be in the hands of Andrea's first husband.

CHAPTER 10

When my mother needed to work out her frustrations, she grabbed a mop and dust cloth and lit into the house. I grabbed gardening gloves and pruners and attacked the yard.

We got back home from Amarillo yesterday and I was still trying to process all the things I learned there; the people I met, the different outlooks and stories they represented. What a tangle Andrea's disappearance was!

And too, I was suffering from jet lag without the jet. Amarillo was a different lifestyle, different surroundings. The weather news said that last night a snowstorm blew into Amarillo, so I was thankful we had made it home before it hit. It sounded like their weather was as changeable as Oklahoma's.

If I had any thoughts of keeping my investigation into the vanished Andrea a secret, those thoughts evaporated after our visit to Dilly's Cafe. So maybe it was a good thing that we hadn't searched out the Amarillo equivalent to Dilly's. We had blown my mental image of a sleuth wearing a trench coat, hat pulled low over her eyes, silently slipping through the darkness to discover hidden clues and bring the bad guys to justice. No, my mother and I had pretty much broadcast to the world that I would be writing a book which just might include a chapter or two about Andrea Worth. So much for secretiveness. We had done a good job of spilling the beans. But when I thought of the hope in Sophie Williams' eyes, it made my efforts worthwhile. She had assured us that she was happy we were taking on Andrea's case. Her innocent trust in my ability made me cringe. Was I worthy of that trust? I hoped so. For Sophie's sake, I would try.

The sun felt warm on my back as I snipped and stacked twigs and branches. Evidently, we were experiencing Indian summer. I viciously cut an offending oak sprout from among the peonies.

And then there was the episode with Grant. It would have helped to have the sheriff of Ventris County on my side but he thought I was a meddling female; albeit, one he was attracted to. I was not ready to become romantically involved with anyone just yet. Jake had been my life and when he died, a part of me died with him. I had grown a protective shell around the area of my heart and I liked it that way. How dare Grant awaken feelings that I wanted kept buried? Whacking off another sprout, I realized, too late, that it was part of the peony bush. And how dare Grant tell me to back off?

With the peonies subdued, I had progressed to snipping the small sprouts around the oak tree when a dark blue SUV pulled into the driveway. A tall, blond man got out of the driver's side and walked to the front gate.

"Darcy? Mrs. Campbell?" he asked. "I'm Gary Worth."

I dropped my pruners and nodded. One of my mother's old sayings came to mind, "Well, speak of the devil." But I didn't say that. I swallowed my surprise and said, "Hello, Mr. Worth."

Gary rested his crossed arms on the front gate. I resisted the urge to tell him he might bend the hinges.

"What can I do for you?"

As he leaned toward me, I noticed that he was a very attractive man. His green, crisply ironed shirt matched the color of his eyes and covered a well-muscled chest and arms. He had the bronzed look of someone who spent a great deal of time out of doors. When I compared Gary with Tom Mott, Tom didn't fare so well. This second husband of Andrea's looked like the proverbial dashing and successful hero of every young girl's dream.

His dark green eyes held mine as he said, "I heard that you are re-opening Andrea's case."

Shaking my head, I said, "I'm not sure what you heard, Mr. Worth . . . ."

A brief smile lit his eyes. "Gary."

"Okay. Gary, I don't know what you heard, but gossip has a way of getting twisted as it goes from one person to the next. I'm planning on writing a book about the mysteries of Ventris County. Much of it will include legends and tales that my Cherokee grandmother told me, and I'll probably have a chapter or two about the Ventris case my mother and I were involved in last spring."

He nodded. "Ben and the lost gold. I've always wondered about that gold and just exactly where it is. Should be an interesting book. So you aren't going to write about Andrea after all?"

I hedged a little. "I don't know yet what will wind up in the book. Sometimes as I write, the story takes on a life of its own and I just sort of record it."

His green eyes narrowed. "That sounds far-fetched to me. You're bound to work from some sort of outline."

I pulled off my gloves and wiped my hands on my jeans. "To be truthful, the story hasn't even reached the outline stage yet. A friend of mine suggested I write a book and include in it some mysteries or legends of Ventris County. Since Andrea disappeared fairly recently and nobody knows where, it might be good to include that. I'd probably use newspaper stories as the primary source."

His eyes never left my face. He seemed to be digesting this. Finally, he spoke.

"I've come to ask a favor, Darcy. Is it all right to call you Darcy?"

"Sure."

"If you decide you need to talk to other people or go searching for clues or whatever, will you come to me first? If you turn up new information, I'd sure like to know about it before I read it in some book. And maybe I can help you. I've still got pictures of Andrea and you'd be welcome to them . . . you know, maybe somebody would read your book and recognize Andrea and realize they had seen her."

That was an angle I hadn't thought of. But then, I hadn't given much thought to Gary Worth as a source of any additional information.

"You're very kind, Mr. Worth, um—Gary."

"Hey, listen, it's been two years. Can you imagine what that's like—the not knowing? I didn't ever think that Andrea was an unkind person, but disappearing like that without even a word; well, that's pretty selfish. Sometimes I lie awake at night and wonder where she is."

He ran his hands though his blond hair and shook his head. He seemed to really care for her. What would make a woman leave this attractive, wealthy man who loved her? That was something I was determined to find out.

"I lost someone I loved, too," I told him. "But it was through death so, no, I can't imagine the pain you are going through. Not knowing has got to be rough."

"We have something in common then. It was nice meeting you, Darcy. Remember to call on me if you need any help at all. I'd like to work with you on finding Andrea. I'm glad that you're writing the book. If we can locate her, even if she doesn't want to come back home, at least I'll know where she is. I'll try to accept her decision and move on with my life."

He gave a brief salute, climbed into his SUV and roared off down the street.

Jethro poked his nose out from under the peony bush. "And what do you think about that?" I asked as I lifted him up. His soft fur felt warm against my cheek. "What kind of woman would leave a rich, handsome man like Gary Worth?"

Once again, my companionable cat had no answers. He sprang from my arms and loped off toward the front porch as if to tell me that he wasn't involved in this dilemma and I was entirely on my own.

CHAPTER 11

Spring Creek, far below me, flashed silver in the moonlight. The flat boulder I perched on had been my seat many times in the past. I walked out here tonight, through Mom's back pasture, hoping the creek and the stillness of the autumn night would work its quieting magic once again. I could think of little else but the mystery of the missing Andrea. During the months since Andrea's disappearance, other things crowded her memory from my thoughts, but since the arrival of Sophie's letter, the mystery and possibilities swirling around her disappearance occupied my mind.

Sophie's letter started the whole thing, at least as far as Mom and I were concerned. The visit to Dilly's Cafe, interviews with Grant and Steve Hopper, the trip to Amarillo and meeting Sophie face to face, Sergeant Romero, Tom Mott, Charlene, all these were like characters in a play. Each one appeared on stage, acted his part, and moved the story along. But in what direction? If answers existed, they were elusive. All I found were more and more questions. Andrea had simply disappeared. It seemed that she was not well loved by everyone. Was she fearful for her life? Had she decided that running away was her only possible choice in order to be safe? And the most unanswerable questions of all: Why had I agreed to help Sophie? What had I gotten my mother and myself into? And why on earth couldn't I learn to let well enough alone?

The tranquility of the night with its elusive scent of water, earth, and small autumn wildflowers began to calm my scattered thoughts. The creek murmured, sleepy insects whirred or clicked nighttime melodies, and a whole family of frogs croaked. These were the familiar sounds of nature before the onset of winter. The silvery moonlight-bathed woods were a balm to the craziness of human tragedies.

Spirit Leap is what the Cherokee people called the sheer granite cliff upon which I sat. A geology professor from the University of Oklahoma once told me that the jumble of jagged rocks along the creek had been spewed from far beneath the earth's surface at some time in the dim geological past. Much more romantic was the old legend that a spurned lover leaped to his death from here many years ago and the earth erupted in protest.

Spring Creek hurried southward, hugging the rocky hillside before disappearing among the trees. Somewhere among those trees, two whippoorwills called, no doubt discussing the departure date for their annual trip to warmer climes. An owl hooted softly and a chorus of crickets announced that autumn was on the way out. Strange disappearances, love, hate, and envy had no part of this quiet autumn night.

An alien noise intruded on the soothing sounds of nature. My scalp prickling, I was at once aware of how alone and remote was my moonlit perch. The sound of dry leaves crunching underfoot jarred me out of my reverie. I patted the pocket of my jeans and felt the comforting bulge of my cell phone.

My boulder chair was at least three feet off the ground and I perched on it like a bird or maybe a sitting duck. Trees and creeks stood out in stark relief under that relentless moon. Without a doubt, I was clearly visible to anyone watching from the cover of those shadowy trees.

Noiselessly, I slipped off the rock and crouched down behind it. I tried to calm my breathing. Surely anyone could hear the hammering of my heart.

An unseen walker moved among those dusky trees behind me. Was it a deer? Possibly a bear? I remembered tales of panthers which were said to live in the area. Or was the source of the sound a person? Grant had warned me that there could be someone in Levi who didn't want me to stir things up concerning Andrea Worth. The night seemed to hold its breath. Not a breeze stirred, but somehow a chill feeling of evil settled over Spirit Leap. What should I do? Should I hide here and wait for whoever or whatever else was out in the night to move on? Should I flip open my cell phone and call 911? Or should I make a run for the house?

Another noise . . . this time an unmistakable footfall and it was closer than the first. I was afraid to raise my head above the rock and look into the woods, afraid of what I might see.

My paralysis suddenly released me and my instinct for self-preservation took over. I sprang up and ran toward my mother's house and safety. Spirit Leap was about a quarter of a mile from Mom's back yard, through an old, grassy pasture that was bordered on two sides by thick trees. I dared not look behind me. My legs burned and I felt as if my heart would burst through my ribs, but I raced like wildfire through the knee-high grass. Something panted behind me, coming closer and closer; or was it my own breathing? I didn't know. Dashing through the backyard gate, I hit the back porch, and hurtled through the kitchen door. I locked it and leaned against it, gasping.

My mother sat at the table, plans for *Ben's Boys* school spread out around her. She jumped up and grasped my arm. "Darcy! What in the world—"

"Somebody—I think was after me," I choked.

"Somebody . . . . Oh, Darcy, I told you I didn't think going out to Spirit Leap was wise. It is so spooky out there. I'm going to call Grant."

I stumbled toward the living room. "Dad's gun. I'm going to get his gun." I yanked open the drawer on the bookshelf and pulled out the black pistol. It felt cold and heavy but reassuring.

Mom's voice came from the dining room as she talked to someone on the phone, presumably Grant. Then she hurried to the front room where I leaned against the bookcase, shaking.

She led me to the sofa. I collapsed on its soft cushions.

"Now tell me what happened," she ordered.

Gasping, I put up a warning hand. "Shhh. Listen. Did you hear something?"

"No, just Jethro crunching his food. Grant will soon be here, Darcy. You are safe now."

CHAPTER 12

My mother poured coffee for all four of us sitting around her kitchen table. Unaccountably, I felt cold. I pulled Mom's old green crocheted afghan over my shoulders, shivering and trying to warm my fingers on the mug.

Grant rubbed his hand over his stubbly beard and leaned toward me across the table. "Darcy, Jim and I have looked all over Spirit Leap and the woods around it and we saw no sign that anybody was there. Are you sure somebody was watching you?"

Jim Clendon, Grant's deputy, drained the last of his coffee and thumped his mug down on the table. "Course, there's not much we can see in the dark, even with that full moon."

"We'll come back tomorrow and take a good look," Grant said.

Clendon frowned. "Look, Grant, what d'you think we're going to find? There's leaves and grass out there. I don't imagine anybody is going to leave a callin' card; do you? And Darcy might have just imagined she heard something. She was out there all by herself; not a smart move, in my book, and her nerves were probably overwrought. Women get that way; overwrought nerves."

I had learned that the chief attribute of Grant's deputy was bluntness; that and a short temper. I had also learned that he did nothing to further my sweet disposition.

"Now, look," I began.

Grant sighed. "It's all right, Darcy. Jim, we'll go back to Spirit Leap after sunup. That's our job. Did you catch a glimpse of anybody, Darcy? Did you see anything at all?"

I shook my head. "No. I just heard a noise . . . two noises. I know somebody or something was watching me."

"Another piece of information for you, Darcy. After you told me about that Rusty Lang, the fellow who threatened you . . . . "

Mom gasped. "Threatened you? Why did he threaten you, Darcy? Why didn't you tell me?"

The adrenalin was draining from my body. Suddenly, all I wanted to do was climb the stairs to my bedroom and go to sleep. "It was a long time ago, Mom, while I was working in Dallas. A picture I snapped of him outside a drugstore sent Rusty Lang to jail for robbery."

She rubbed the deepening wrinkle between her eyebrows. "I didn't know that being a newspaper reporter was so dangerous."

"What about Rusty Lang, Grant?" I asked.

"I checked with Dallas," Grant said. "Lang served his time and is out on good behavior. And, Darcy, this is what's really important—he was sighted here in Levi."

The swallow of coffee lodged in my throat. "Here? Why is he here?"

"That's what we asked him when we cornered him in Dilly's Café. He said he's here visiting his cousin," Grant said.

Jim snorted. "Huh! Cousin, my eye. He's no more visitin' his cousin than . . . . "

I was getting sleepy in spite of the coffee. The feeling of relief at being safe and the warm afghan caught up with me. My eyes felt like lead.

"That's okay, Grant. I needed to know. Now, if you two gentlemen will excuse me, I've got to go to bed. Jim, maybe I am overwrought, as you say. But I know what I heard and I know that whatever it was, it wasn't friendly."

CHAPTER 13

Why do you run away from problems, Darcy? Nobody spoke these words aloud but I heard them in my mind as clearly as if Granny Grace were sitting beside me in my red Ford Escape. Granny died when I was only ten years old but during those ten years she was my best friend and confidante. And, although I didn't want to think I lacked courage, she was right. When Jake died, I ran home to Mom. After the trip to Amarillo, I went to my "thinking spot" at Spirit Leap. And now, after last night's scare, I was running again, this time to Granny's land along the Ventris River where she once lived. Maybe it was the old "fight or flight" dilemma, and since I didn't know who or what to fight, I chose the other option.

But today I wanted to hear the sound of the wind in those giant trees, to smell the freshness of the river, and to feel the peace of nature's beauty. I needed to think about Andrea and her mother and Gary and Tom and Charlene. And then there was Grant—I should face my feelings for him and his for me, but I was actually afraid to look at them squarely.

All these thoughts and emotions churning and swirling through my mind needed to be sorted out. In the quietness and stark beauty of my grandmother's home, maybe her serene spirit would calm me. The land she had loved seemed the best place to go when my own spirit needed to feel her presence.

A few dark clouds were gathering in the west and brown leaves on the trees crowding the road shivered in a brisk breeze. Indian summer never lasted long and a cold front probably lurked just beyond the horizon.

Something slithered across the road in front of me. I rolled down the window to get a better look.

A rattlesnake! Of course, I knew these hills sheltered many animals, but it wasn't often that these reptiles came out of hiding. This one, though, seemed to have some place to go in a hurry.

Mom offered to come with me this morning. She had, in fact, insisted. It was a good thing she hadn't come. Seeing the rattlesnake would have made her want to turn around and go back home, even though we were safely ensconced in my car.

"I've just got a bad feeling, Darcy," she told me this morning. I understood, because an elusive apprehension clouded my own mind, but I laughed at her premonition and finally convinced her I needed some time alone after last night's trauma. So, after promising I would check in with Pat Harris at Ben's farm and soon-to-be-school which was on the way to Granny's land, she said no more.

I was as curious as my mother to see what progress had been made on the Ben Ventris farm and school. Hiram Schuster, a longtime friend of my parents, oversaw the work going on. Pat Harris would be the cook and she had definite ideas about what renovations the kitchen would need. Hopefully, her plans and my mother's would coincide.

But more important to me was simply clearing my mind of fear and bewilderment. I could almost convince myself that the sounds I heard last night were simply my overactive imagination. Deep inside, though, I knew the noises were menacing. Somebody had watched me from the obscurity of the woods. And I thought someone had followed me back to my mother's house. If I hadn't been such a coward, I would have turned around to see who was behind me, but I didn't. I had focused on getting to safety as quickly as I could. Perhaps the breathing I heard had been my own. Maybe the watcher had stayed in the woods.

My childhood memories of times at my grandmother's home were of peace and safety. Each time I returned to the land, I seemed to feel the joy and serenity of my Granny Grace. Going back now, even though Granny and her house were gone, still gave me the same secure feeling I had as a child. Today I needed to be there.

The dirt road narrowed at the bottom of a hill. The tires of my Escape crunched on the gravelly bottom of a small stream that flowed across the road. Water splashed against the car's underside as it crept through the shallow creek.

A low roar started somewhere back in the woods. I jumped and gripped the steering wheel. What was happening? A tree crashed across the road in front of me, some of the limbs brushing my car's hood. At the same time, it felt as if a giant hand shook the Escape. I lurched forward, banging my forehead on the steering wheel. Something weird was moving, something violent. I turned off the ignition and grasped the door handle. Should I get out of the car? Should I not? The ground under me shuddered and the rutted road heaved up and down as if a giant snake slithered beneath the surface.

The rumble stopped as suddenly as it began. No wind stirred the leaves now. Nature seemed to hold her breath. What had happened? Slowly, the truth dawned on me. An earthquake! Incredible, but true. I had never experienced one, but there was no other explanation. Somewhere in the depths of the earth, an unstoppable force moved and nature bent before it.

My car door did not want to open and my arms seemed to have turned to water. After three tries, I was able to creep out of the SUV. I clung to it for support. Drawing a ragged breath, I pressed my palms together to stop their shaking. The tree blocked the road in front of me, but behind me the road looked clear. Backing up was my only option until I could find a spot wide enough to turn around.

Then a terrifying thought hit: earthquakes don't happen in isolation. Levi itself was bound to have been shaken. And Mom—what of her? Was she and her house safe? I started to climb back into my car.

"Miss Darcy! Wait! Don't go!"

The sumac bushes parted and a large young man rushed toward me.

I rubbed my eyes. "Jasper? Jasper Harris, what in the world are you doing out in these woods?"

"Never mind that," he said." We've got to get to that school of Ben's. My mother is there. We just had an earthquake—did you know that? I didn't know we had earthquakes around here. Maybe Mom was hurt. Come on. We've got to hurry. Now, Miss Darcy. You're wastin' time." He trotted to the passenger side of the car and opened the door.

I slid back behind the steering wheel. "In case you didn't notice, Jasper, that tree is bigger than we are. I don't think I can plow through it."

"Never mind," he said, his voice an octave higher than usual. "Back up. There's an old wagon road down there a piece. I know a shortcut to the school."

Putting the SUV into reverse, I inched back the way I had come.

Jasper pointed to a wide spot between two trees. "There it is! Turn right there."

Visions of scrape marks along my new car passed before my eyes. I was particularly careful with it since my old one took a tumble down Deertrack Hill last spring. So far, the shiny paint of this car bore no scratches. I wanted to keep it that way.

I shook my head. "Jasper, that trail is fine and dandy for skinny wagons and horses. If you'll notice, this Ford is a bit wider and I have no intention of putting creases in it."

He grabbed the door handle. "Well then, scoot over and let me drive."

Was he serious? I snorted. "That'll be the day."

We crept along the old ruts, limbs brushing metal. "Please Lord," I prayed. "Just get us safely through."

Jasper frowned at me. "Hurry up, Miss Darcy. Go faster. I could run this fast."

I gritted my teeth. "Be my guest."

Jasper pointed out the side window. "That there's a shortcut to the Worth ranch."

Leaves had nearly covered the faint marks of a trail. "How do you know that, Jasper?"

He pointed to his head. "I know lots of things that nobody else knows. It's best to keep some things a secret. Safer."

"What things? Why do you say that? Do you know something about the Worth family?"

Who was it suggested I talk to Jasper? Somebody at Dilly's?

He shook his head. "Hurry, Miss Darcy. The school is just up ahead."

The roof of Ben Ventris's old barn appeared through the trees. I turned in the direction Jasper pointed and was in the Ventris pasture with the house a short distance ahead of us. The buildings all looked intact to me, and when Pat came out on the porch to hug her son, she confirmed that there had been no damage. "Just some paint cans knocked off shelves and a scared cook—me! Darcy, you go on home and make sure Flora is all right. Jasper, you ride home with me. I hope my house doesn't have cracks in the foundation. Earthquakes in Oklahoma! Heavens! What will happen next?"

That was a question I didn't ask any more because it seemed that another disaster lurked around every corner, waiting to pounce.

Taking Jasper's shortcut might be quicker than the roundabout way of the county road. At least I knew there were no trees across the old wagon rut. I couldn't relax until I knew my mother was unharmed. Since everything at the Ventris farm was safe, hopefully the buildings and people in Levi were all right, too.

Whispering a prayer for Mom's safety, I headed back through the woods the way Jasper and I had come.

The clouds had gathered forces and a light rain fell as my car eased through the shadowy woods. The headlights beamed a tunnel through the crowding trees. Out of the corner of my eye, I glimpsed something; a long, tawny brown something which glided directly into my path then stopped and turned its head toward me. The lights of the Escape glinted on yellow eyes.

My heart turned over and my breath caught in my throat. I was looking at the biggest cat I had ever seen. A snatch of remembered conversation with Amy came to my mind: "animal legends . . . panthers in the thickest part of the woods."

In front of me stood one of those legends. My hands shook as I checked my doors to be sure they were locked. For a few seconds the cat stared at the car, then with the infinite grace of the wild, he sprang into a thicket and vanished. An unearthly scream rose and fell from a hidden spot among the trees. My scalp prickled and the hairs rose on my arms. Many years ago my dad told me that the cry of a panther sounded like the blood-curdling shriek of a woman. He was right.

My breath coming in short gasps, I gripped the steering wheel with sweaty palms. I always drove carefully, taking care not to stress the engine, but at that moment, all I wanted to do was leave these gloomy woods behind me. I gunned the motor and bounced over that trail probably faster than anybody had ever traveled it. Upon reaching the road, I broke all speed limits getting back to the safety of civilization.

CHAPTER 14

"Darcy, this is all so unbelievable." Coffee sloshed from her cup as my mother raised it to her lips.

I nodded. "Yes. First the earthquake, then the mountain lion. I can tell you that my heart was in my mouth when that thing turned and looked at me. And that scream! It made my blood run cold."

My mother shook her head. "You know, Darcy, we are not to believe in superstitions. That would be wrong. God is much greater than all the evil in this world."

She traced a small crack in the top of her antique dining table. I knew that thoughtful look. "But? Out with it. What superstition are you talking about?"

"Oh, you know all the silly things about breaking a mirror or a black cat walking across in front of you," she answered.

"And about owls being harbingers of good or bad luck. Yes, I remember. But that isn't what you're talking about, is it?"

Without looking up from that mesmerizing crack, she said, "I was just remembering what my mother, your Granny Grace, said about the scream of a mountain lion."

"Granny Grace was a Christian, Mom. Surely she didn't put any stock in old wives' tales."

"No, she didn't. But she said there was a saying among some people that the cry of a panther meant death."

A finger of fear traced itself down my backbone. That was understandable. Never in all my life had I heard anything so otherworldly. Taking a sip of coffee, I considered. "Well, I believe we can disprove that one. Although it scared me, that wild cat didn't threaten me at all. He just hid in the bushes."

Mom nodded. "Yes, that's what he did. I imagine the earthquake had upset him and maybe put him on the prowl. You know, animals can sense an earthquake or a storm coming before it actually happens. Maybe that panther was out at Spirit Leap last night. Maybe that was what you heard in the woods."

A panther? Well, why not? If it, with its finely tuned wild senses, knew that the earth was about to shake, it could have been nervous and moving around. But the footfall I heard didn't sound like the quiet padding of a cat. It was too loud for that.

"Have you heard any local news tonight about the earthquake?" I asked, going to the television set.

"Actually, I haven't thought of that! I guess the quake rattled my nerves and then I was worried about you."

"It looks as if it's big news," I said, as a picture flashed onto the screen.

The TV anchorman stood by a large map of the United States. He was introducing a prominent seismologist.

"Quakes that can be felt in Oklahoma are relatively rare," the earthquake expert said, "but they certainly happen, ten times more frequently than usual since 2009."

"So does Oklahoma sit atop a major fault?" Drew Adamson, the anchorman, asked.

"Pressure can build along fault lines," seismologist Charlie Thomas answered. "The Wizetta Fault, or the Seminole Uplift as it is called, is a very deep fault east of Oklahoma City."

"The quake was felt over much of the central and northeast parts of Oklahoma," Adamson said, indicating bright little dots along the state map. "Reports are coming in from Oklahoma City all the way down to Tulsa, Tahlequah, and Levi."

"We will hope this is not a "forequake," Thomas said. "That is a sort of pre-earthquake that comes before a much bigger one."

"Oh, my goodness!" Mom said. "Turn it off, Darcy. We certainly don't want an earthquake bigger than this one."

I obliged and poured another cup of coffee.

"You know, Mom," I said, "that mountain lion didn't seem threatening, but he might have a taste for domesticated meat if he could find it. I think you or I had better tell our neighbors about my encounter with it. Their horses and mules might be in danger, although I guess the panther would have to be awfully hungry to jump on something as big as a horse."

She snapped her fingers. "Oh, I almost forgot. Grant phoned. He asked that you call him at the office when you got back. He wants to know that you are safe, I'm sure. And he asked if the quake had damaged anything. I told him the only damage was to my nerves."

I fidgeted. Should I return Grant's call? I didn't want to encourage him, but I wanted him to keep the lines of communication open in case he found anything else about Andrea Worth, or if he and Jim discovered some sort of proof at Spirit Leap that would make my story about a noise sound more like truth and less like hysteria.

The note of relief in Grant's voice was unmistakable. "I'm glad you're all right, Darcy. Earthquakes are something we don't know much about here in northeast Oklahoma," he said. "We usually know when a tornado is headed our way but an earthquake . . . ."

He was probably sitting at his desk shaking his head. "Do you remember that heavy old file cabinet in my office?"

"Uh-huh," I answered.

"The quake scooted it away from the wall and left a crack in the ceiling. Anyway, Darcy, it's great that you and Miss Flora are safe. I want you to stay that way. Which leads me to the next thing. Jim and I checked out the woods and pasture at Spirit Leap this morning before the quake and we didn't find anything, but remember that Rusty Lang is on the loose again and I don't think he has any particular love for you, Darcy."

So much for finding proof that Jim Clendon was wrong about my overwrought nerves!

Grant paused. "Are you really sure that you heard something in the woods last night? Do you think it might have been just a deer?"

The feeling of being watched was real. If Grant believed Jim rather than me, though, there wasn't much I could do to change his mind. However, I wouldn't give Grant the satisfaction of hearing my story about the mountain lion. Then he would be certain the wild animal was my noise in the darkness.

"Oh, Grant, I don't think so, but who knows? By the way, Rusty Lang shouldn't be a problem. After all, I didn't make him rob that drugstore. He simply paid for a wrong decision. Surely he doesn't hate me."

"I wouldn't count on it, Darcy," Grant said. "Criminals have to blame somebody. Think about it. He is from the Dallas area, so what's he doing in Levi, Oklahoma? I doubt that he came up here because of a fondness for his cousin. Just keep your eyes open and don't go anywhere alone."

Grant might be the sheriff of Ventris County, but the last time I checked, he didn't have the right to give orders to a law-abiding citizen. I bit my tongue. "Okay. I'll be on the look-out," I replied sweetly.

I hung up and saw that Mom was gazing at me with an expression that could only be called "extreme motherly concern."

"Don't worry, Mom; a person can't go through life in a glow of love and friendship. Probably everyone gathers a few enemies along the way, but we don't always know who they are. See how lucky I am to at least know about Rusty? I can be on guard now."

She just looked at me and shook her head.

I walked over to the coffee pot. Good. There was enough for one more cup. "You know, Grant said that earthquake moved a file cabinet in his office. Could it have shaken up things at Spirit Leap? If we went back and looked, maybe we could find some kind of clue that Grant and Jim overlooked. I really believe someone was out there with me at Spirit Leap last night. I could sense it."

Mom frowned. "If you are thinking about going back to that dangerous place, I can tell you right now that I'm going, too. Not today though; it's too wet and dreary. What do they call those earthquakes after an earthquake?"

"Aftershocks."

"Yes. Well, who knows? We might have one of those aftershocks. You could meet anybody or anything out there. Until we know that you are no longer in harm's way, wherever you go, I go." She nodded her head.

Sighing, I said, "And put you in danger too? I can't see that'd help me."

My mother lifted her stubborn chin. "Wherever you go, I go. Period."

"Yes ma'am," I said meekly.

CHAPTER 15

The sky shone a sunny blue and all I needed was a light sweater across my shoulders as my mother and I walked through her back pasture to Spirit Leap the next morning. Nature seemed to be apologizing for the earthquake and dismal rain of yesterday. I could almost believe, along with part of a poem by Robert Browning that "God's in His Heaven; all's right with the world." But, sad to say, although He is, it isn't.

The boulder that had been my chair didn't look right.

"Look at that," I said. I dropped down on my knees. "You can see where the rock used to sit; there's mud beside it instead of grass. The earthquake must have moved it!"

Between the grass at the bottom of the rock and the rock itself was a muddy strip of bare ground about two inches wide which ran the length of the boulder.

My mother joined me on the grass. "You're right. That's a slide mark. I can't believe it! This thing must weigh a ton."

I put my hands against the side of the rock and shoved. It didn't budge. "I can't even begin to imagine the force that could scoot a monster like this," I said.

Sunlight glinted upon a metal object at the base of the rock. I picked it up. A black and silver pocketknife lay in my hand.

"Well, well. What have we here?" I held my open palm out to Mom. She touched it with one finger.

"A knife! Was it under the rock?"

"No. It was in the grass on the edge of this bare strip that the quake uncovered."

"Why didn't Grant or Jim find it? It's pretty big. I don't see how they could have missed it."

"Somebody could have been out here after Grant and Jim left." I shuddered. Why would anybody trespassing on my mother's land come to this particular spot?

"Maybe Grant came back later and looked again to see if he could find any sign of an intruder. Grant himself could have dropped the knife," Mom nodded. "Yes, I'll bet that's what he did."

I turned the knife over. On its side were a few letters. "I'd say this thing has seen some heavy use. Looks like there used to be a name here but it has been rubbed off." Four dim letters: C, H, m, s were in faded silver against the black knife.

"It looks like something that may have been used as a promotion; a sales gimmick. Or maybe a door prize from a store that was having a sale. Those items always had the name of the store that was promoting it imprinted on the side. I remember your dad carried one for many years from Sutter's Hardware. Joe Sutter gave them to his customers after he remodeled and had a grand opening. It had *Sutter's Hardware* on the side."

"But who dropped it? Was it Grant or Jim? It could have been a hunter who dropped it a long time ago. This is deer season; maybe someone stopped here at the rock to wait for a deer to come out of the woods."

Mom nodded. "I'd hate to think anyone would go hunting here without asking my permission but that's a possibility, too."

She got to her feet. "Well, hand it over to Grant. Let him try to figure this out. I hope there's nothing sinister about its being here. It could have been here for years, hidden in a crevice of the rock. It just took a good hard shake to jar it loose."

If it comforted my mother to think that, so be it. I closed my hand around the knife. "If I take it to Grant, you can bet that he's not going to be happy when I tell him we were back at Spirit Leap. He doesn't want me to try to play detective."

"If you are thinking about keeping this a secret, forget it. If there really was someone out here last night, maybe he dropped the knife. Maybe it's got fingerprints on it or something. You shouldn't keep it, Darcy."

My mother was right, but I dreaded taking the knife to the Ventris County sheriff. If I asked around town, at Sutter's or one of the other stores, would I get any information? It seemed unlikely that asking questions about where the knife might have come from would shed any light on whoever was here last night. I was convinced somebody had been watching me. But who? And why? Was Grant right about my not getting involved in Andrea Worth's disappearance? Seemed to me I was pretty much in the middle of things already.

As we walked back to the house, my mother echoed my thoughts. "Darcy, I've been thinking. Just suppose there really was someone here last night; was his purpose only to scare you?"

"If that's what he meant to do, Mom, he certainly succeeded."

"Or did he mean to do more than scare you but you outran him?"

I pulled my sweater tighter around my shoulders. "I don't know."

"No, of course you don't. But think, Darcy, why would anyone want to do either; why would he want to scare you or do you harm?"

"I guess there're only two possibilities: Rusty Lang who is out for revenge or somebody who doesn't want me to meddle in the disappearance of Andrea Worth."

"There's another possibility," Mom said, as we went through the backyard gate. "What if Andrea is alive somewhere and for whatever reason, she wants to scare you off because she just doesn't want to be found."

"What if. . . . " Why hadn't I thought of that? "Why would she do that?"

"Only one reason I can think of . . . she's happier away from Levi and has no wish to come back home or she's afraid to come back."

"But wouldn't she at least have told her mother that she's alive?"

Mom rubbed her forehead and gazed off into the distance. "Not if she feared for Sophie's safety, too."

I wished at that moment that Cliff Anderson had not placed Sophie's letter in Mom's mailbox. If only he had misplaced it or lost it along his route. But he hadn't. Cliff was a very conscientious mail carrier. But if he had lost that letter, I could be reasonably sure that Rusty Lang was my only enemy.

CHAPTER 16

A slightly past-forty face with high cheekbones, longish hair, and dark eyes gazed at me from the mirror. And between those eyes were two frown lines. I could lay these most recent lines squarely at the door of our local sheriff who politely blew his stack when I took the pocketknife to him.

"I thought the knife might belong to you," I said demurely.

"No, it doesn't belong to me and Jim Clendon doesn't carry one."

Amazingly, he did not seem at all pleased with my thoughtfulness although he did say the knife looked somewhat familiar.

"Weren't you listening to me, Darcy? Haven't you learned from experience that there are people in this world who wouldn't mind diminishing Levi's population by one nosy reporter who can't seem to understand that pure evil exists in this crazy world?"

He had slammed the knife into his desk drawer, muttering something about the probability of smeared fingerprints, and the wisdom of staying away from Spirit Leap. I fled Grant's office like a scolded child. Where was my backbone?

Enough of that! It was a good thing that I had made a picture of the knife with my digital camera. The picture showed all the details, including the letters and the spaces where the letters had been rubbed off. I didn't tell Grant but it seemed to me that the quicker the mystery of Andrea Worth was solved, the faster I would be safe. I had already put out feelers about her disappearance and I didn't know how to back out at this late date. As for pure evil—yes, I was quite sure it existed. It seemed that much of it had settled in Levi, for some strange reason. I also believed that "greater is He that is in me than he that is in the world." I would just trust Jesus for my safety and do my best to find out if Andrea Worth was dead or alive. Whichever it was, I needed to know. And the only way I knew to ferret out her whereabouts was to ask questions. First stop would be the hardware store to see if Mr. Sutter could identify the knife. But that was for another day. This day had been stressful enough and I was ready for the rest that my neatly turned-down quilt and sheets promised me.

"Scoot over, Jethro," I told the sleeping cat. I bent down to scoop him off my bed and deposit him on the floor. Suddenly he sprang up on stiff legs, his back arching and the fur along his backbone standing straight up.

I jerked my hands away and stared at him. Never, in the two months since he had adopted my mother and me, had he behaved this way. My throat felt tight. "What's wrong, old fellow?"

The cat didn't appear to be looking at me. Instead, he gazed at the opaque night outside my bedroom window. His wide, unblinking yellow eyes brought back the memory of my encounter with his wild cousin. My legs suddenly felt like rubber.

Tiptoeing to the light switch, I flicked it off. Moonlight filtering through the large window silvered my room. When I glanced again toward my bed, Jethro was nowhere in sight. I moved quietly, hardly daring to breathe. Something had caught the cat's attention; something that I had neither seen nor heard. I brushed the curtain aside and peered out. Below me, the peony bushes in the front yard bowed their stalks to a brisk breeze. The limbs of the oak swayed above the gate. I strained my ears and heard nothing but the rattle of dry leaves. Then I heard something else—a muffled thud that was different than the usual night sounds.

My mouth felt dry. Was that a footstep on the front porch? Should I wake Mom? Should I phone Grant? I pulled the curtain across my window. Had someone been down in the yard watching to see when I turned out my light and went to bed?

Jim Clendon's words came back to me about women and overwrought nerves. I would not call Grant again unless I had proof that my nerves were not the culprit.

I crept into the hall. Gentle snores came from Mom's room. Inching down the stairs, I prayed that the third step from the top would not creak as it usually did. The wind moaning around the corner of the house was the only thing I heard on the first floor.

I thought of Dad's old pistol in the bookcase drawer and willed my bare feet to cross the hall floor into the living room. Sliding open the drawer, I pulled out the gun. It felt cold and heavy but reassuring.

No intruder in his right mind would ever enter a house where there was a nervous woman and a gun. The muscles along my shoulders felt as tight as the wires inside my old upright piano. Even though I held the gun with both hands, it jerked up and down in a spasmodic dance. Should I call out that I was armed and dangerous? I had a mental image of flinging open the door, squatting in a classic "gotcha covered" pose and yelling . . . yelling what? If someone was out there, did I want to hold him until help arrived or scare him away? I took one small step toward the door and rammed my foot against the rocker part of my mother's rocking chair. Pain ricocheted through my big toe. I yelped and dropped the gun. It went off with a boom that vibrated through the house. Something thudded on the porch followed by a short scuffle; then, silence.

In that shocked quiet after the gunshot, my mother clattered down the stairs. "Darcy! What happened? Did someone shoot at you?"

I pointed to my gun lying on the floor by the door. "No, I thought I heard someone outside and then I whacked your rocking chair and dropped the gun and it went off."

She grabbed my arm. "Someone outside? Are you sure? You could have been killed, Darcy, by your own gun. Oh, for goodness sake! Thank the Lord you're safe."

"No, Mom! Don't do—"

Too late. She unlocked the door, flung it open, and flicked on the porch light. Nothing moved in the yellow light. No shadows crowded in from the darkness.

She pointed to an empty flowerpot which rolled against a porch post as the wind moved it. "There's your prowler, Darcy. And I don't think it is dangerous at all."

I pushed the door closed, re-locked it, and sank down on the floor. My legs wouldn't support me any longer. Okay, maybe there was no one on the porch. But what had Jethro sensed? Would something as innocent as a windblown flowerpot cause that terror-stricken stare?

And would I ever feel safe again?

CHAPTER 17

What little sleep I got the rest of that fractured night came in snatches, punctuated by dreams of being chased by faceless intruders. By 5 a.m., I could stand no more nightmares. I dragged myself out of bed, slipped into my jeans and a red T-shirt, and staggered downstairs to plug in the old yellow coffee pot. By the time I had washed my face, brushed my hair, and fed Jethro, dawn was a faint glimmer in the east.

Surely, if there had been someone outside our house, the gunshot had scared him away. Yet, as I stepped onto the back porch, a feeling of fear met me. Overwrought nerves again? Drat that Jim Clendon! I found myself second-guessing every emotion, wondering if my nerves were playing tricks on me. Did I hear or only feel something stirring? The world still lay in pre-dawn grayness although the eastern sky promised the sun was back there somewhere, waiting to slip above the horizon.

The air felt odd, heavy, and damp as I took a deep breath and tried to banish the jitters.

Wispy clouds in the west shone a little lighter than the rest of the sky. Were they harbingers of one of Oklahoma's infamous tornadoes? But it really wasn't warm enough for that. Maybe the woods were on fire farther south. Even though the smoke was not visible, it sometimes added a thickness to the air. I sniffed. No, I couldn't smell wood smoke. Somehow, though, the morning felt different. Perhaps it was the leftover dregs of my scare last night. Or maybe it was all in my sleep-deprived brain, my overwrought brain.

Mom had apparently not slept well either. She came out of the house behind me and sniffed. "Thought I smelled smoke. You are up early, too. I tell you, Darcy, I don't know what to think about the noise you heard last night. I don't know if all that excitement or this oppressive feeling in the air is what kept me awake."

I turned to kiss her cheek, but she was frowning and squinting toward the west. "You think a tornado's brewing?"

We lived right in Tornado Alley where some of the nation's most vicious storms arrived regularly, especially in the spring and fall. I shook my head. "I don't think so."

She voiced my own appraisal. "Somehow it just doesn't feel like tornado weather."

Something moved in the pasture on the north side of our house. Our neighbor's mule lived there and recently two saddle horses had arrived to keep him company. The horses trotted to the fence and whinnied softly to us then suddenly wheeled and tore across the field, heads up and tails streaming behind them, as though a pack of wolves were in hot pursuit. The mule trotted out to meet them and split the morning with his raucous bray.

"What's got into them?" Mom asked.

"Oh! I'll bet that panther is around. He must be scaring them!"

Mom groaned. "Oh, no. I forgot to call the neighbors to warn them to keep an eye on their livestock."

As we watched, the horses reached the corner of the pasture near the woods and ran straight toward the barbed wire fence, skidding to a stop in the nick of time. They reared and squealed, then raced on down the fence line toward their barn.

"I don't know. They seem to be really scared. Maybe that wildcat caught a calf or jumped onto one of the horses."

We went down the steps and around the corner of the house to watch such strange behavior on the part of these usually gentle animals. Still squealing, the horses and mule ran into their barn and immediately began to kick the sides of the wooden structure. A loud crash came from the far side of the building.

Mom grabbed my arm and pointed. "Look at that, Darcy." Three deer shot out of the woods behind the back pasture and headed toward our garden fence. Deer were common along the river and in the woods behind the pasture, but they didn't usually stray from the cover of trees during the day. This bunch, however, ran with their heads up, white tails flagging an alarm. They sailed over the garden fences with room to spare, one after the other, then flashed across the road and into the brush beyond. A big doe, fifty feet behind the others, tried to jump the fence, stumbled and fell on the rough garden area. She righted herself, bolted across the garden, sprang over the outside fence, and charged directly toward the road at the front of the house. She did not seem to see the truck headlights that beamed down the road leading to Levi.

Mom grabbed my arm. "My lands! That truck's going to hit that poor thing for sure!"

But the driver saw the doe in time and veered toward the ditch, barely missing her.

"I've never seen deer or horses act so crazy for no reason," Mom said. "It must be the panther but I don't know where it is. I certainly haven't seen it."

Looking back in the direction from which the deer had come, I couldn't see anything unusual. And neither Mom nor I had heard the panther's spine-chilling scream.

The doe tumbled into the brush, and the lumber truck pulled back onto the road and kept going. One second the truck's headlights beamed a straight path through the murky morning; the next, they jiggled up and down like the scenes in an old movie.

Far back in the woods, a cracking sound began and grew into a roar. The trees in the yard shivered as if they felt a sudden chill.

The ground shuddered beneath our feet. Everything around us shook as though a high wind were striking the area. Behind the house, something banged and crashed. Glass rattled and splintered with the tinkle of a thousand icicles.

Mom gasped and wheeled back to the porch. She slipped and landed hard on one knee. "It's another earthquake! We better get inside before it gets worse!"

I dropped down beside her and grabbed her arm. "No, we are better off in the open. Your poor knee, Mom. It's bleeding."

I had an unreal feeling of déjà vu. That first quake must have been a preview of the coming attraction because this one was a doozy. I heard Mom whispering, "Heavenly Father, protect us . . . ."

The trembling lasted for perhaps a minute. I hadn't realized I had closed my eyes until it was over. I opened one eye at a time, fully expecting to see our house in shambles. But the home that had stood for a hundred years still appeared intact so far as I could see in the growing light of morning. A filmy cloud drifted over the tops of the trees in the back pasture. Smoke? Dust? Whatever it was, I hoped it didn't signify disaster.

Mom struggled to get to her feet. "I've got to take a look around and see how much damage has been done."

"Let's wait just a little longer. Sometimes aftershocks immediately follow a quake like this."

For another five minutes, we sat on the ground, expecting to feel the shaking again. An eerie quiet settled over everything but the earth remained still and solid. As the sky lightened further, we could see a large tree near the corner of our property lying partly in the road. The big corner fence post leaned toward us, kept from falling only by the wire nailed to it.

My voice sounded as shaky as I felt. "I wonder what happened to the truck we saw heading toward town?"

Cautiously, we got to our feet. Mom gingerly touched her knee. "Do you reckon anything inside the house is broken?"

"Well, things look pretty normal from here, but let's walk around the outside first and . . . oh, no!"

The house had originally been built with a big chimney on the side that ran up both levels of the structure and extended about six feet above the roof to allow escaping embers from the upstairs fireplace to cool before falling onto the flammable roof. But now, instead of the tall red brick four-foot square chimney, there was only a jagged stump. In the growing light I could see a few loose bricks lying across the shingles. Several large chunks of red brick were scattered in the yard, twenty feet from the side of the house. The mortar was old and had obviously crumbled, so most of the bricks had broken apart before falling to the ground. A crack ran down one side of the stump that was left intact. A huge chunk had broken off and fallen in against the other side, sending two slabs plummeting to the ground. Several small pieces of brick and mortar lay scattered across the yard.

A few steps closer we got an even bigger shock. A pair of jeans-clad legs stuck out from under the biggest chunks. The jeans ended above tan western boots. One foot pointed at the sky, the other pointed downward.

CHAPTER 18

My mother dropped to her knees. "Oh my Lord, Darcy." She grabbed my arm with fingers that felt like steel bands. "There's a man under there. Our chimney fell on somebody. Who is it? What was he doing here? We've got to get him out from under that thing and to the hospital."

Surely Mom and I were caught in some sort of a dream from which we'd soon awaken. The downed tree, the toppled chimney, and now the partially hidden man under a pile of bricks seemed like last night's nightmares merging with reality. I knelt beside my mother.

"Yes, we need to get him out and we'll have to have some help to do that, but I really don't think there's anything a doctor could do for him."

The upper half of the body lay hidden under the broken chimney. There was no way two women could lift that pile of bricks.

Surprisingly, the cell phone in my pocket worked and my numb fingers punched in 911. Even more surprisingly, after only two rings, a gravelly voice answered. Roy Peel, Mom's neighbor who owned all kinds of farm equipment, was manning the phone.

"Roy, we've got an emergency here. Our chimney fell on somebody; I don't know who, and we can't move the bricks and stuff off him. We need an ambulance and probably we need Grant, too. Hurry, please."

"Right. Help is on the way, Darcy, but it may take a while for the sheriff to get there. That quake might have downed some trees across the road."

Mom looked up at me as I ended the phone conversation. "Darcy, go check in the house. I'll stay here beside this poor soul. I couldn't make it inside anyway; my legs are too shaky."

My legs weren't in the best working order either and my hand, as I patted her shoulder, shook like the oak leaves above us. "I'll hurry, Mom."

I dreaded what I might find inside. Another dead body? Had the house been damaged to the point that it would topple over on us? Astonishingly, except for minor damage, everything in the house seemed to be okay and no one else, alive or dead, was in sight. Some small glasses in the china cabinet lay in shards on the floor and the big Monet print of spring violets that had hung in the dining room for years lay face down on the table. The quake had tumbled cans of food onto the floor but these things were the only visible damages. Possible structural harm to the interior walls, plumbing, and heating, would have to wait for a more experienced eye than mine.

I ran back to the yard. Mom still sat beside the pile of bricks and mortar. My nerves were jumping so that I could not sit still so I began picking up and tossing broken bricks and glass out of the path leading to the front gate.

"I hear them coming," Mom said. A distant wail grew closer. The ambulance stopped in front of the gate, its siren moaning into silence. Two EMTs hopped out and hurried toward my mother and the body. They looked at the debris covering the victim. Ted Everett, one of the attendants, turned toward me. "More help is on the way. There's a lot of junk on this poor devil. You got any idea who he might be?"

Mom and I both shook our heads.

A county truck equipped with a winch and two burly men screeched to a halt behind the ambulance. The taller man shook his head. "Terrible thing. Here, Joe, back right up to the fence and lower that cable. We'll have him uncovered in no time."

"Not that it'll do much good," Joe muttered.

In less than three minutes, the cable was lowered, the huge hook latched onto the largest chunk of mortar, and the powerful winch motor whirred. Just as the slab was about to be raised, a white Ford Ranger pulled in behind the tow truck. Grant and Jim Clendon sprang out.

Grant took in the scene and turned to me. "Was this person a visitor? Somebody who was coming or going? Or did you even know he was anywhere around?

I shook my head. "We had no idea, Grant. We just found him after the quake." I felt my stomach clench.

"Are you and Miss Flora okay?"

"Yes, Grant, but that man . . . ."

He gave my shoulder a brief pat and watched as the cable slowly lifted the chunk of our chimney off the person on the ground.

I turned my back on the scene and covered my face with my hands. Thankfully, Mom had moved to the corner of the yard and faced away from that prone figure. She had no desire to see what lay under the debris and neither did I.

Grant spoke gently. "I'm sorry to ask this, Darcy, and I am pretty sure about who he is, but I want you to look at this fellow and tell me whether you know him."

He kept his arm around my shoulders as he led me up to the poor man on the ground. I took a deep breath and looked. His head had been turned to the right when the chimney fell and now his face was toward me. His hair was dark, his nose was long, and there was a scar just above his left eyebrow. There was no doubt I had seen this man before—in a courtroom in Dallas, during a trial in which I had provided photographic evidence. Was he the noise I had heard last night? Had he been in our yard all night or had he left, scared away by my gun and come back this morning? I would probably never know. It looked like he had been out for revenge. There was one thing I did know: the sad story that began in Dallas had ended here with Rusty Lang dead at my feet, a lethal-looking rifle beside him.

CHAPTER 19

In thirty seconds the EMT's confirmed my first impression that nothing could be done for the man on the ground. "He died when the first big chunk from the chimney hit him," Ted Everett said.

Then Everett turned to Grant. "We'll finish up our report and get out of here, but I guess you'll want to leave the body until the medical examiner arrives?"

Grant nodded. "Yes. I've already contacted the morgue."

My mother made a choking sound and stumbled toward me. "Oh, Darcy. If that quake hadn't happened when it did . . . ." Unable to continue, she began to cry. "That man, that Rusty Lang, had a rifle. Do you think he meant to shoot you? The earthquake broke our chimney, but it looks like it saved our lives and at the same time, killed that poor soul there." Mom's eyes were wide and she was pale and trembling, obviously near collapse.

Everett cleared his throat. "Maybe we ought to take a look at you two ladies. Sometimes a person gets hurt in a disaster like this and doesn't realize it until after things have calmed down."

Over Mom's head, I nodded at Ted Everett. "It might be a good idea if you took a quick look at her. She stumbled and fell on one knee when the quake first started and I'm afraid her blood pressure is going to be sky-high."

As Everett reached for his medical bag, I took Mom's arm, then he and I led her toward the wide front porch and lowered her to the first step.

Grant pulled his cell phone from his belt, punched in a number, and spoke quietly. Putting his arm around my shoulders, he drew me close. "I'm thankful to the good Lord that my two favorite women are not harmed. Yes, Lang must have been out to get you. What other reason could he have for being here with a gun? A close call but that's all it was. He won't be a threat any longer."

Amazing how good it felt to lean against Grant with his strong arm around me. For a few seconds, I closed my eyes and tried to block out the horror of the morning.

Joe worked the hook off the fallen slab of bricks and signaled the truck driver to re-wind.

"Sheriff, if you won't be needing us any longer, we'd better be getting back. I'm betting we'll have more work than we can handle today," he said.

Grant nodded. "Yes, I'm sure you will, but the last word I got was that the damage wasn't as extensive as it could have been." His gaze swept up and down the jagged pile of bricks. "I'm a little surprised there wasn't more harm done to Miss Flora's house considering the way this chimney cracked wide open."

Jim Clendon squinted up at the roof. "Maybe the chimney was already cracked from that first quake. And anyhow, it was old and the mortar was most likely brittle and didn't need much shaking to break."

Grant nodded. "That's probably the case. But since the house was built originally on a tall foundation, I think it would be a good idea to have an expert take a look at the underpinnings before long."

He nodded to Joe and his helper. "Thanks a lot, boys. We may need a statement from you later, after the medical examiner has taken a look at the body, but I'll get back to you if we do."

I was sitting on the porch steps watching Ted Everett bandage Mom's knee when Lieutenant Dave Swearingen from the Oklahoma State Police arrived. He got out of his car, shaking his head. "I would have been here sooner, but things are pretty bad just south of here. There's a lot of trees down and that Quik-Mart at the corner of Hazel and Oak is in shambles. I had to take a detour and come down Highway 82 because the main roads are mostly blocked. But so far, I haven't heard of any casualties." He gestured toward the man on the ground. "Except this one. I won't be surprised, though, if there're more. A search crew is out right now."

"What about the bridges?" Grant asked.

Swearingen shook his head. "All okay so far as I've heard except for the one over Spring Creek. Seismologists pegged the quake at about 6.5. They say the epicenter was way south of us, in an area of open fields, and that limited the destruction that might have occurred if it had smacked Levi right along Main Street."

Swearingen took a laptop from his car. "The medical examiner will want to take a look at this guy, but we don't need an expert to tell us what happened here. All we need now is confirmation of his identity."

He opened the laptop, knelt beside the crushed body, and lifted one of the dead man's hands flat against the computer screen. "I've already called headquarters and they've got somebody waiting to compare these fingerprints with the ones we have on file."

It took less than five minutes for the message to appear on the screen. *Confirmed. Rusty W. Lang, dob: 02/27/81. Convictions on record for theft, breaking and entering, assault, violation of probation and numerous juvenile charges.*

"You knew it was that Lang person right away, didn't you, Darcy?" Mom asked.

I nodded. "I'll never forget how he glared at me in the courtroom. He really hated me for taking that picture. I guess he meant it when he said he'd get me."

"Is my mother okay?" I asked Everett, who was putting his tools back into his bag.

"She's going to have a walloping bruise on that knee and you were right about her blood pressure. I gave her a pill that'll help her relax. She ought to go in and lie down. That med will make her kinda shaky."

Grant and I held onto Mom's arms and helped her up the steps and across the front porch. But before we got inside, she turned to Grant and gave him a look that seemed not at all affected by the tranquilizer. Her speech didn't seem slurred either.

"Grant Hendley, now that this man is dead, is my daughter safe and we can breathe easy?"

He patted her hand. "I think you can relax. You sure won't have to worry about Rusty Lang anymore."

I noticed he didn't really answer her question.

We walked her to her bedroom and slipped off her shoes and tucked a quilt around her shoulders. I kissed her forehead. "Rest a little now and when you get up, things are going to look a lot better."

She looked up at me. "Is that a promise?"

"Sure, Mom. That's a promise."

Grant went with me into the kitchen. A glance at the old oak cabinets brought me up short. They appeared to be slanting toward the northeast corner of the kitchen, and there was a crack between the largest one and the kitchen floor. I tried to open the lower cabinet door where we kept the coffee. It stuck. Grant moved around me, put both hands on the door and pulled. The door came off and he sat down suddenly.

I giggled. "Sorry, Grant. You just looked rather surprised."

Grant grinned. "That's how I felt, too. Anyway, it's off and it'll stay that way for a while."

Mom and I had been debating the wisdom of trying to remodel and update the old house. My mother wanted to stay where she had lived for forty years, but I believed a new house would be more comfortable and convenient for her. The earthquake had most likely resolved the matter.

"It looks like the quake gave the kitchen a whole new look," I said, reaching for the can of coffee.

He took the can from my hands. "I may not make a cup of Joe that equals Miss Flora's, but I've had lots of practice. You sit down and I'll do the honors."

"You'll get no argument from me," I said. "If I ever yearned for a cup of hot, bone-jarring caffeine, it's now. Thanks for being here."

"I'll go soon—it's going to be a long day. But first, we both need something to settle our nerves. In lieu of anything stronger, I hope this coffee fills the bill. I imagine that lieutenant out in the yard could use a cup too."

A white van from the Ventris County Morgue was pulling up to the gate as Grant and I walked back into the front yard. I carried a cup of coffee to Lieutenant Swearingen who was sitting on the porch, busily entering data into his computer.

Hopping out of the van, a white-coated attendant opened the hatch and pulled out a gurney. Doc McCauley alit from the passenger side and bustled toward the body. He nodded to Grant and me. "Grant. Darcy. Miss Flora okay?"

"She will be a lot better after her nap," I answered.

"Well, bring her in tomorrow and I'll take a look. You too, Darcy."

As well as his small black medical bag, Richard McCauley always brought with him a sense that things were going to get better. He knelt beside Rusty Lang. "Darcy, you are going to have to find a new profession," he said.

"You don't care for my newspaper stories, Doc?"

"Your writing is fine. It's your nose that's the problem."

"You don't like my nose?"

"It looks all right but you're always sticking it into trouble. You've gotta stop that."

Grant raised an eyebrow. "That's what I keep telling her."

Dr. McCauley might be reassuring, but he was also blunt. And it looked like he was right.

"I'm done here." He snapped his bag shut and grunted as he got to his feet and dusted off his knees. "Take care, Darcy. I'm serious," he said over his shoulder as he followed the gurney with its burden back to the van.

"Hey, Doc, got a minute?" Lieutenant Swearingen intercepted him as he turned toward the gate. Jim Clendon joined them.

Grant took my hand and led me away from the porch, toward the peony bush by the front gate. His tone was somber. "I need to talk to you, Darcy."

"It's not really over, is it, Grant?"

"I'm afraid it may not be. I don't know. You see, I think Rusty was out for revenge, pure and simple. But I think you've stirred up a hornet's nest with your investigation into the disappearance of Andrea Worth. We haven't resolved anything there. Haven't found Andrea, haven't uncovered anything about what might have happened to her. I think you'd better be very cautious and watch your back, Darcy."

This was sounding more and more ominous. A hornet's nest was a pretty apt description. I had a mental picture of a swarm of those angry little yellow insects zeroing in on me. But at least a person could see the hornets coming and I had no idea who my enemies were.

My mouth suddenly felt dry. "Okay, Grant, let's assume that somebody who doesn't want me nosing into the Andrea business hired Lang; maybe Andrea herself hired him, if she's still alive and doesn't want to be found. Maybe Lang wasn't out for revenge. Maybe he was just trying to carry out orders."

Grant ran his hand through his hair and took a deep breath. "Think about it, Darcy. It makes a whole lot more sense that Rusty Lang had planned to get even with you the whole time he was locked up. I doubt that Andrea or anybody else hired him. It's a possibility, but I think he acted on his own. I doubt very much that just because Lang is dead, you are no longer in danger. I think somebody in Levi doesn't want you snooping around the Worth case and that person is still very much alive."

The horror of what he was saying felt like somebody had punched me in the stomach. "So, it may be that Rusty wasn't my only enemy? There may be somebody else out there who just doesn't like me very much?" I gulped.

Grant nodded. "Maybe."

"And you think that maybe he or she is still determined to . . . um . . . silence me?"

Grant's mouth tightened into a thin line. "Could be."

Once again I wished that our mailman had lost Sophie Williams' letter. I wished I had turned a deaf ear to her plea. I had not only opened myself up to danger, I had put my mother in danger, too.

"But Grant, you are just guessing. I really think that Rusty was my only immediate worry. With him gone, I don't think there's anybody else who would be willing to commit murder. That's a dangerous thing in itself. Nobody ever gets away with taking someone else's life. Most people draw the line at that. Anyway, most sane people do."

Grant was silent, staring off down the road. Finally, he muttered, "You just said it, Darcy. I agree—most sane people would never attempt to kill another human being. But what if there is an insane person in town who is just unbalanced enough to think he could get away with it? What if he has weighed the risk of getting rid of you against the possibility that you might find out what happened to Andrea? Maybe the stakes are so high that he is willing to take that risk."

I shook my head and shivered. The morning sun was doing nothing to dispel the chill in the air.

"You must have a guardian angel, Darcy Tucker, watching over you. I just hope he's always there when you need him."

I was so near tears that I couldn't even correct him. Tucker, Campbell, whichever, I had never been so afraid in all my life. And yes, I believed in guardian angels. Mine must be very busy.

CHAPTER 20

The aroma of freshly brewed coffee greeted me as I came downstairs the day after the earthquake, but that was all that was normal about the morning. My mother stood in front of her sink looking at the dilapidated cabinets with tears in her eyes. I saw no sign that she was preparing breakfast.

I put my arm around her. "It's a real mess, isn't it?"

She nodded without speaking.

"Why don't we have a cup of coffee to sort of get our eyes focusing properly and then go to Dilly's for breakfast?"

She sighed. "That's about the only thing to do, Darcy. Everything inside the house is torn up and I don't really have the heart to tackle it. Maybe I'll feel better after some of Artie's pancakes."

"And, Mom, if the inspector says there has been extensive damage to the foundation and supports, it might be a good time to think about moving to a newer house, don't you think?"

Mom glared at me. "Now Darcy, we've been all through this. The house is old but then I'm no spring chicken any more either. Would you want to throw me out if I had a car wreck and needed a lot of expensive surgery? No? I don't want to throw out this old house either. I've got a lot of good memories of your dad wrapped up within these walls."

Was there ever anybody as hardheaded as Flora Tucker?

Much of Levi must have had the same idea we had, because the parking lot at Dilly's was full. Thankfully, the cafe looked intact. A fallen tree lay near the parking lot. I would guess it had once been across the lot but had been dragged away to make room for customers. Artie waved us to a booth that had just been vacated. Tony wiped off the table and with a flourish handed us the breakfast menu.

"Glad to see you two are all right," Tony said. "Levi was lucky that we didn't have more damage. There's a crack running up the wall of the kitchen but that's all we've seen, so far."

I sat down and relaxed. I loved this place.

We were halfway into our pancakes when Zack Crowder ambled over to our booth. I smiled at this young man who was a third or fourth cousin, I wasn't sure which.

"Darcy, Aunt Flora, do you mind if I sit down?"

I scooted over to make room. "Would you like some coffee? I don't see much of you anymore. Your mom said you are driving a truck. Who are you driving for?"

Zack frowned. "I drive for this one and that."

Tony came by with the coffee pot to refill our cups. "Gary Worth, is who I heard," Mom said.

I popped another bite of crusty brown pancake into my mouth. "Your mother was worried about you the other day. Do you drive out of town?"

He was silent and Mom tapped my foot with her toe.

I shook my head at my mother. So, okay, maybe it was a nosy question but a reporter had to be nosy, didn't she? However, I didn't want Zack to be offended and leave in a huff. "Sorry, Zack, curiosity of the reporter."

"That's okay. I wanted to ask you, Darcy, if you're going to go ahead with that book."

"Well, sure I am. Why would I not?"

"Oh, I don't know. Sometimes people around here get kind of nervous when reporters start asking questions." He twisted a high school class ring on his left hand.

"Surely nobody would object to answering questions if they have nothing to hide."

"Darn it, Darcy, some of the people in town think that you're going to be sticking your nose in where it doesn't belong. Why can't you just let well enough alone?" Zack asked.

What was it about my nose? Doc McCauley had objections to it too.

Zack was shredding a paper napkin. "It stands to reason that if you are getting involved in another police matter, you might be putting yourself in danger. I heard talk about a dead guy being found squashed outside your house after the quake. Rumor is that he was carrying a gun."

Suddenly Dilly's pancakes lost their flavor. Dilly's must surely be the most efficient purveyor of information in the whole state. How under the sun did Zack already know the details of Rusty Lang's death? And if Zack knew, his mother knew, and Earlene Crowder considered it her civic duty to pass along every juicy tidbit that fell upon her eager ears.

Zack slid out of his seat and stood looking down at me. "Why can't you just be happy with helping Aunt Flora and puttering around your yard? You don't need to be doing any writing about Levi. Folks around here are kinda private."

After he left, I looked over at my mother. A frown creased her forehead. "I'm not much hungry any more, Darcy."

"Nor am I. Let's go, Mom."

"I need to run across to the grocery store. I'll be along to the car in a few minutes," she said. "There's a food sale going on 'cause a lot of canned stuff was dumped on the floor. If the cans aren't actually dented or damaged, I don't mind buying them."

I was so lost in thought as I left Dilly's that I almost bumped into one of Levi's oldest and most colorful characters. Burke Hopkins put out a hand and grabbed my arm. "Whoa there, Darcy. I didn't mean to run into you."

I grinned and shook his hand. "Mr. Hopkins, it was my fault. I should have watched where I was going." I had always admired this man. My dad used to say there wasn't a person anywhere more honest than this old gentleman who stood smiling in front of me.

Burke Hopkins was Cherokee. Although I had not seen him for about ten years, his brown leathery face looked the same as I remembered. He had to be nearly ninety because he had two sons who were in high school with my mother and she was 67. He let go of my hand and heaved a case of Dr. Pepper into the back of the truck parked at the curb. He had evidently been to the grocery store, too.

"How are you, Mr. Hopkins? You don't look a bit older than you did the last time I saw you."

He chuckled. "Oh now, I bet you learned how to make an old man feel good while you were down there in the big city. Why, I've got a birthday coming up and I'll be 89." He stepped back onto the sidewalk. "Actually, you don't look a bit older than you did the last time I saw you either. I think you must have been about 16."

I laughed out loud. "If I looked 16 the last time you saw me, it must have been 25 years ago!"

Although his father had been half Cherokee and half Hispanic, Burke Hopkins was clearly the son of his Cherokee mother. With his hooked nose, prominent cheekbones, and the still-thick snowy hair, he was the kind of man who stood out in a crowd. His bushy brows were black as a crow's wing and his narrowed eyes were the color of tarnished copper. Time had not bent his broad shoulders. He would retain his dignity and character as long as there was a scrap of Burke Hopkins.

I noted his scuffed boots, blue jeans, and red plaid shirt, faded as was the man who wore them, but impeccably clean and well fitting.

"Are you still living in that pretty white house south of town?" I asked.

"Oh yes, with Wolf and Ranger. I've got those old dogs beat as far as age goes but they're sharp as tacks, don't talk back to me, and tell me if a stranger is coming. Now who could ask for more?"

"Sounds like the best of worlds to me. You used to keep a flock of hens, too."

He nodded. "Still do. I sell the eggs at the farmer's market every Saturday. Course, the quake might have put them off their egg laying for a spell. It sure riled up my two old dogs."

His deep voice softened. "I was sorry to hear about your husband dying, though, Darcy. Bad trouble, that."

I swallowed the painful lump that clogged my throat at the mention of Jake. Hurriedly, I changed the subject. "I can remember when you and my dad used to go fishing together and stay on the river all night."

He nodded, and pushed his old black Stetson away from his forehead. "Yes, and then we'd build us a little fire out of tree branches along the creek and fry up some catfish and perch for breakfast."

Hopkins patted my arm then stepped back a little and his big, warm, calloused hand slid down my arm and folded around my hand. For a moment we stood on the sidewalk together, remembering the past.

Suddenly he seemed to freeze as an odd expression creased his face. His black brows v'd down over his nose and his eyes seemed to look through me and not see me. He clasped my other hand at the wrist and his fingers tightened like a vise, so hard that my watchband bit into the flesh. Was this man having a stroke right before my eyes? When he spoke, his voice was coarse and grating, not at all as he normally sounded. "Darcy, I've got the strongest feeling that you're in danger. What are you getting yourself into?"

If somebody had dashed me with a bucket of ice water, I couldn't have been more chilled. I tried to jerk my hands away but he held on. I licked my lips. "What . . . why do you say that? What are you talking about?"

He seemed to come back to the present with a start. He dropped my hand and stepped away. "I didn't mean to scare you. Not a bit. But sometimes I just know things and I know that you might be looking at some mighty dangerous times ahead of you. Watch your step, Darcy."

Burke Hopkins hurried to his truck, climbed into the driver's seat, and roared off down the street. I stared after him, not moving. The goosebumps on my arms had nothing to do with the temperature. The old man's words were ominous. Had he heard about Rusty Lang who had been killed under our window by the earthquake? Or did he have a sixth sense, as Mom said my Granny Grace had? It seemed that everywhere I went, somebody was warning me of possible harm. Surely I could do something about it and not just wait for the other shoe to drop. But what could I do? I certainly wasn't asking for danger.

In my heart I knew this wasn't perfectly true. I hadn't been coerced into finding out what happened to Andrea Worth. I could have told Sophie I wouldn't do it. Zack and Dr. McCauley were right. My curiosity often led me to places I probably should not go. And now there was Burke Hopkins' warning. I had better do something fast. If I could find out what happened to Andrea Worth, surely there would be no more danger coming at me from any direction.

CHAPTER 21

The "something" I decided to do was go and see our family friend and Levi's most popular lawyer, Jackson Conner. I deposited Mom and the sack of groceries in the kitchen of her house, then started back out the front door.

"Where are you going, Darcy?" she asked.

My mother meant well and truly was concerned for my safety. I had not told her about Burke Hopkins' warning, nor did I intend to. I believed in "Least said, soonest mended." Or, in this case, least said, fewer explanations I would have to give my anxious parent.

"I just want to think about a few things, Mom. No need to come with me. I may see someone I know downtown." This was basically true.

"Do be careful, Darcy, although I'd feel a lot easier in my mind if I went with you."

I ruffled her short curls. "My bodyguard. Thanks, Mom, but I'm sure I'll be fine."

Gazing at me thoughtfully, she said, "I pray that you will be. Anyway, Grant said he thought when that Rusty Lang person died, that took care of any crazy person who wanted to hurt you."

Hopefully, Mom would keep believing that and perhaps she was right, but I was afraid that until Andrea's disappearance was solved, the danger would exist.

The sign read *Jackson Conner, Attorney at Law*. I maneuvered my car into an empty parking space and slid out of the leather seat. His office mirrored the character of Jackson Conner. The cedar paneling, brown leather sofa and chairs, and framed photographs of local places of interest exuded an aura of strength and stability. As I walked in, the aroma of cherry-flavored pipe tobacco met me. That scent was what I remembered most about Jackson Conner.

His receptionist was not at her desk and the attorney himself opened his inner office door. He came toward me, hand outstretched and smiling.

"Darcy Campbell! What a pleasant surprise on this gloomy old day. What can I do for you?"

"I'm not sure, Mr. Conner. Just a talk, I guess. Do you have time?"

"I've always got time for Flora Tucker's daughter. How is she?"

He gestured to the chair in front of his desk. I sat down and noticed he still had that comforting plaque on the wall, *If God brought you to it, He will take you through it.*

"My mother is fine, thanks. Her house suffered some damage in the last earthquake but, thankfully, we are both all right. I guess you heard about the man found in our yard?"

"That I did. Also heard about your fright out at Spirit Leap."

Why should I be surprised at that? But I wondered who found it newsworthy enough to pass along to an attorney.

"I'm wondering, Darcy, if it has to do with the book you are planning on writing? Heard about that, too."

Grinning, I said, "One of the benefits of a small town is that we could do without modern means of communication. Levi's gossip is faster."

In a courtroom this man would be a formidable figure. His thick shock of white hair, handlebar mustache, and blue eyes that seemed to demand "the truth and only the truth" might have been the pattern God used when he made old-time, straight-as-an-arrow lawyers.

Jackson Conner would not appreciate my beating around the bush so I came straight to the point. "What, if anything, have you heard about Andrea Worth's disappearance? Do you have any idea what could have happened to her? Did she leave under her own steam? Or was there foul play? What do you think?"

Jackson smiled and reached for his pipe that was on an ashtray in front of him; the pipe that reminded me of one I had seen in movies about a 19ᵗʰ-century English sleuth. "I do keep my ear to the ground, Darcy, but I'm not clairvoyant."

He lit his pipe and cleared his throat. "However, you may not know this, but Andrea Worth was a client of mine. That is, I guess she would have been."

If I had been blessed with antennae, they would have quivered. "No, I didn't know. You see, Mr. Conner, Andrea's mother, Sophie Williams wrote to Mom and me. She asked if we could help her reach a conclusion as to what happened to her daughter."

He leaned back in his chair and drew on his pipe. "Hmm. That is indeed interesting."

"Nobody knows about the letter except Sophie, Mom, a friend in the OSBI and me. Even Grant Hendley doesn't know. I'm hoping you keep this information to yourself."

"Of course. I wonder, though, if it is wise for you to stir things up. There are some things going on in Levi that shouldn't be going on in a small town, nor in any town, for that matter. You realize, I hope, that there are forces of evil in this old world and when those forces feel threatened, they lash out. I'm afraid our sheriff and his deputies are hard-pressed to rid our town of some mighty foul goings-on."

Another warning. And another mention of evil. "I remember that Grant said there is a drug problem. Is that what you are talking about?"

"Yes, that is what I am talking about. Illicit drugs are coming into Levi from somewhere, but where? That's what's keeping our sheriff and others in law enforcement awake nights. But getting back to Andrea: when she came to see me, she was a scared little thing. She came to me shortly before her disappearance. She wanted to talk to me about divorce."

I gulped. "From Gary?"

"From Gary. I'm not betraying client/attorney privilege, Darcy, because my client is not here and I fear she is dead. At any rate, I'm telling you this. She wanted to know about her many assets, how to keep Gary from getting half since he had very little at the time of their marriage. This was her second marriage, you know. But she never did carry through. I figured she and Gary patched things up."

A smoke ring drifted lazily to the ceiling as I considered this. So Andrea wanted a divorce. If she died or disappeared, Gary would have control of all of Andrea's assets. This was certainly something to think about. But, if she died, Charlene would have better grounds for demanding her right to Inglenook Ranch. And, if Charlene married Tom Mott, Tom would at last have his hands on all that land. It looked like several people would profit from Andrea's death.

"I have the letter that Sophie wrote," I said, rummaging in my purse. "I'd like for you to read it."

As I pulled out the folded paper, a photo copy of the mystery knife fell out onto Jackson Conner's desk.

He picked up the letter, read it, and handed it back to me. "I see. So I guess you and Flora felt it was your duty to help this poor woman. What's this?"

He picked up the knife picture and studied it.

"I found the knife at Spirit Leap, the day after the first earthquake. I don't know how it got there or who may have dropped it. Have you ever seen a knife like that?"

"Oh, yes. It looks familiar. I just can't recall where I saw it yet. I will though. Hmm. Some letters on the side are missing. I'm guessing it was a logo for a business."

"That's what I think, too. I've been planning to show it around town and ask if anyone can tell me about it, but with all the excitement from the earthquake, it slipped my mind, or didn't seem that important."

"Where is the actual knife?"

"Grant has it."

"Then let him do the asking. I'm going to repeat, Darcy, that you must be very careful. Asking questions of the wrong people can be dangerous indeed."

CHAPTER 22

I climbed back into my car and sat for a few minutes, thinking about my conversation with Jackson Conner. The day seemed to be getting colder, and although it was noon, the sun was nowhere to be seen. All these warnings were beginning to fray my nerves. I have no more courage than the average person, and in the light of all the warnings about evil and danger and keeping my eyes open, perhaps I should call Sophie and tell her that I was going to turn the whole thing over to Grant and let professional law enforcement people try to solve Andrea's disappearance.

Then I thought of Sophie's troubled face. I could almost hear her saying that she had already tried professional law enforcement and they came up with a big, fat zero.

People closest to the victim were always the first suspects and judging from what Jackson Conner had to say, all was not well in Andrea's marriage. But OSBI agents, the Ventris County sheriff at the time, and anyone else with a badge had swarmed all over the Worth home and they all came up with nothing. In their depositions, more than one witness swore that no vehicle had entered or exited the Worth ranch on the day that Andrea supposedly disappeared. Surveillance cameras Gary had aimed at his house showed no unusual activity. The film captured nothing suspicious.

Okay, Andrea vanished so she had to get out of there some way. The question was—how? What other person could I talk to who might hazard a guess as to how an average-size young woman could have vanished like snow in sunshine? The owner of a dairy just down the road from the Worth ranch reported that he got up before daylight to milk cows. He had seen no vehicles go past his home in the pre-dawn darkness. If Andrea were afraid for her life and wanted to leave without anyone's knowledge, what baffling method did she use for accomplishing that?

Would she simply have walked away? Did she know the thickly forested area around her home well enough to thread her way through those woods and hide in a cave or a sheltered glen? But, where would she have gone from there? Sooner or later, she would have come out and tried to find more a more permanent hideaway.

What would I do if I wanted to run away from a threat? Would I think that disappearing without a trace would bring safety? I would probably need an accomplice; but what trustworthy person could I turn to? Who would keep a secret like that, no matter what the consequences? And who might know a secret way out of the Worth property?

It would have to be someone as stoic as Jasper Harris. Jasper! Like a light bulb coming on, I remembered his words the day of the first earthquake when he and I had taken the wagon road to my mother's farm. He had pointed to a spot between two trees and said that was a shortcut to the Worth Ranch. Then he refused to tell me anymore and said it was better to keep some things to himself.

Was Jasper ever interviewed concerning Andrea's disappearance? Probably no one could lay hands on him to ask him any questions. But Jasper was the one person who roamed the woods of Ventris County and knew them as well as he knew his own home.

I should just call Jasper and ask him to show me that dim path again. Or not. Did I know that I could trust Jasper Harris? What if he had done something to Andrea, either accidentally or on purpose? If he knew the shortcut to Andrea's home, had he used it for nefarious purposes? I had witnessed Jasper's temper in the past. Could he have lost his temper with Andrea for something trivial or important, at least in his eyes, and lashed out at her in anger?

Starting my car's engine and putting it in gear, I drove slowly down the street. Maybe I could find the shortcut myself. A real downer, though, was that evidently an elusive but dangerous panther considered the area his own private stomping grounds. I was not eager to meet up with that long, graceful cat with the blood-curdling scream. But I could drive out that way and stay in my car. Perhaps I would get an insight as to how Andrea could have left by this little-known route. Mountain lions were shy and stayed away from people. Surely it would not attack me if I were in the Escape.

I called my mother. Her answering machine came on. Good. "Eat lunch without me, Mom," I said. "I'll be along soon."

That little chore taken care of, I headed out of town in the direction of Granny Grace's acres.

When I arrived at the old wagon ruts, I pulled my SUV off the road as far as possible and squinted into the dense growth of trees. I couldn't see any sign of the shortcut Jasper had pointed out.

There was nothing to do but retrace the way I had gone when Jasper rode beside me. Easing the car between two saplings, I inched along the track made by horses and wagon wheels, many decades earlier. Where were we when Jasper pointed out his side window and said, "That there's a shortcut to the Worth ranch"? Then he had shut up and refused to say more.

Creeping along, scanning the woods to my right for any sign of a break in the trees, I wished for a powerful spotlight. The branches of towering oaks and sycamores met in a canopy overhead obscuring most of the light from the shrouded sun. There! That had to be the path. Dense trees and undergrowth parted for a good way back into the woods, marking a faint trail. It was not wide enough for a car or truck, but an ATV could squeeze through, surely.

Shutting off the engine, I scooted over to the passenger side of my car. There was nothing but dark trees and bushes as far back into the woods as I could see. I fumbled in the glove compartment, got out the flashlight and opened the door. The dim circle of light did no good at all. If I got out and walked through the woods, maybe I could find something if I knew what I was looking for. Maybe I would see a button, a piece of jewelry—anything that did not belong.

However, the Escape offered safety from the wild critters who lived here. What if I happened to meet another of those wild relatives of Jethro?

"Please, Lord, give me Your protection," I whispered. I remembered someone saying a long time ago that the Lord protected fools but I didn't think that was biblical.

Looking back at my vehicle after venturing away only two steps, I nearly changed my mind. It represented safety and civilization. I would go only a short way, scanning the area with the flashlight, and if nothing turned up, I would go home. There was only the smallest of chances that something lost two years ago would still be visible. Two seasons of brown leaves would have covered any evidence at my feet. Even though the chances of seeing something suspicious were remote, the memory of Andrea's anguished mother acted as a spur. I determined to search, futile though it might be.

Something dangled from a blackberry bush a few steps ahead of me. I hurried forward and shone my light full on it. Reaching through the thorns, my searching fingers touched the hard, ridged object. I drew it out for a closer look. A clump of dried berries, fused together as they grew, lay in my palm, hangers-on from last season's crop. Some clue! It was not much of a reward for scratched fingers.

With no warning, thunder crashed over my head. I must have jumped three feet into the air. Rain followed on the heels of the thunder, pelting me with hard, cold drops. When my heart slowed to normal, I glanced back for the comforting sight of my SUV. All that I could see were trees and more trees. Without meaning to I had come far enough to lose sight of my Escape. I would have to depend on the flashlight to guide me back to the dim trail and shelter. Beaming the light at the ground, I realized that rain-darkened leaves all looked the same. I faced the nerve-jangling truth; I was lost.

Surely my Cherokee forbearers had left an ingrained sense of direction somewhere within my genes. Taking a few steps to the right, I squinted through the rain. A sumac thicket barred my way. I turned to go the other direction and a scattering of gray limestone rocks blocked my path. I took a deep breath, trying to slow my heart to normal.

My ancestors may have roamed these woods without ever getting lost, but somehow that enviable skill had not filtered down to this descendant.

Lightning sliced through the darkness followed by another deafening peal of thunder. I yelped and scooted under an oak that still had a lot of brown leaves on its branches. Maybe it was foolish to be under a tree with all the electricity sizzling through the air, but since the trees were as thick as the fur on my tomcat's tail, I decided I would be as safe under one as not.

The only thing to do was wait out the storm. When the sun shone again, at least I would know east from west. Surely I could see something familiar to guide me back to my car. My cell phone! I patted my pockets but could not feel that comforting bulge. With a sinking feeling, I realized the phone was in my purse and my purse was in the car. Crouching close to the tree trunk, I tried to shield my eyes from the blinding rain.

After 15 minutes, I had had enough of waiting for the storm to abate. If anything, it had gathered strength. Standing up, I shouted as loudly as I could, "Help!" So much for dignity and my reputation. I cared for neither. All I wanted was to be in the shelter of my beloved car and on my way back home.

Who but a foolish and nosy crime reporter would be out in the woods on a day like today? People with any sense were safe at home. Undoubtedly, the only ears near enough to hear me were those of forest dwellers. I yelled again.

Something rustled in the bushes. I gripped my flashlight, ready to wield it as a weapon. I might not be a match for a panther but I determined to die fighting.

Lightning lit the trees and bushes around me, and a tall form stepped from the curtain of rain.

"Miss Darcy?"

Jasper dodged a tree branch and stopped in front of me. I grabbed his arm as if it were a lifeline. "Am I glad to see you!" I yelled above the sound of the downpour.

Jasper sidled closer. "What under the sun are you doing out here, Miss Darcy? Of all the goofy things! Are you lost?"

I gulped. "You might say so."

Then I noticed the rifle cradled in the crook of his arm.

I pointed to the gun. "What are you doing out in these woods, in the rain, Jasper, with that gun?"

"I was squirrel huntin' before the storm caught me. I do that sometimes. Oh, for Pete's sake! Don't you know better than to be out in the woods during a thunderstorm? Where's your car, Miss Darcy?"

"It's back on the wagon road, wherever that might be. That is, if it hasn't been washed down the hill by a flash flood."

His words were edged with irritation. "You have no business out here. What if I had thought you were a squirrel or a deer and shot you? You hadn't oughta be out here. It's way too dangerous."

He grabbed my hand and tugged me along with him. I had to run to stay up with his long strides. My red car was a beautiful sight as it emerged from the trees. Jasper opened the door and practically shoved me inside.

My teeth were chattering. "Can I give you a lift back home, Jasper?"

"No. I've got other things to do. Just remember what I told you. Stay out of the woods. Don't come back in here again, Miss Darcy."

CHAPTER 23

My mother waited for me inside the front door of her farmhouse.

"Darcy Campbell, you look like a drowned rat! Where in the world have you been? I was so worried. Go get into some dry clothes and then wrap up in an afghan while I get you something hot to drink."

I obediently went to my room, opting for pajamas and a robe as the long autumn night would soon be closing in. I sat down in the recliner in front of the cold fireplace, draped Mom's green afghan around my shoulders and closed my numb fingers around the cup of steaming coffee she brought. I wished we had had the chimney repaired. A crackling fire would be welcome now. Jethro jumped up on my lap, turned around twice and nestled into the afghan. Ah! The comforts of home. Now and then it was nice to be fussed over.

The telephone shrilled in the kitchen and I heard Mom hurry to answer it. Draining the last drops of coffee, I set the cup on the floor, and closed my eyes. Rain drummed a lullaby on an overturned flowerpot on the back porch.

Shutting my eyes, I leaned my head against the soft chair. Jethro's hypnotic purring became the sound of my mixer as I stirred up a chocolate cake in my home in Dallas. Jake came up behind me and put his arms around my shoulders.

I smiled. "You aren't helping me get this cake in the oven."

But, before he could answer, Mom shook my shoulder. "Darcy! Darcy, are you awake?"

I opened my eyes as Jake and the kitchen in Dallas disappeared. "I am now, Mom."

"That was Sophie on the phone. She was pretty upset about a troubling development."

What about this case wasn't troubling? I set Jethro on the floor and tossed back the afghan. Whatever the information Sophie had, I hoped it was important enough to have interrupted my pleasant dream.

Mom poured dry cat food into Jethro's bowl. "Sophie said that Tom Mott is going ahead with the fence. Remember he had the posts and the wire there in that area near where we ate our lunch on the Inglenook Ranch."

I nodded. "It seems to me that Tom is needling Sophie. If that land is legally hers, she can certainly make him take down the fence."

"Yes. She realizes that, but she will probably have to go to court or at least ask the sheriff to take care of it."

"I think she should file harassment charges," I said.

"She may. He just sounds like a thoroughly disgusting character. He told her that as soon as he marries Charlene and Andrea is declared legally dead, the ranch will be his anyway."

"I'm afraid he'll have to wait five more years unless Andrea's body turns up before then."

Mom looked down at Jethro who had spurned the dry food and was winding figure eights around her ankles.

I bent over to stroke his back. "Spoiled cat! I'll have to mix some canned food with the dry." Jethro followed me to the cabinet as I reached in for a can of his favorite food.

Mom sighed. "It's nearly time for our supper, too. How does cornbread and milk sound to you?"

"Perfect."

"Good. And while we eat, you can tell me where you were and how you happened to get soaked to the skin."

I would tell her about getting lost in the woods and being rescued by Jasper but I knew what her reaction would be. "Darcy Campbell, surely you know better than to go poking around in dark woods where panthers live. What on earth were you thinking?"

What indeed? When my mother and I took on the mystery of the missing Andrea, I had no idea we were opening the door to a whole slew of questions, suspicions, and dangers. But, we had taken this assignment and there was no backing out. Somehow, I must discover what happened to Andrea Worth.

CHAPTER 24

That night I lay in bed and watched the clock creep toward one a.m. Ironically, I had come home to Levi in May for rest, peace, and healing after Jake's death. So far, the peace had eluded me. As for the healing— well, if I were honest, I would say that I could look at the loss of my husband a bit more calmly now, but I also had to wrestle with guilt. If several hours passed without the pang of loss stabbing my heart, I felt guilty. In fact, rarely did I get to sleep before midnight.

Last spring, Mom and I had been enmeshed in the drama concerning Ben Ventris and who had killed him. And now, only a few months later, here we were again, neck-deep in trying to figure out what had happened to Andrea Worth.

At night, when all the busyness of the day should have been laid to rest, my mind kept swirling. Where was Andrea? How could we find out what had happened? And, judging from all the warnings I had been getting, how wise were we to continue?

But there was another key figure in this drama, for a very different reason—Grant Hendley. I would have to be blind not to know that Grant still loved me. And, as disloyal to Jake as it seemed, I could not push away all those long-ago memories. Grant's and my romance had continued for three years. After we both got out of high school, we had looked forward to a future together.

I well remembered the night we sat in his old Chevy truck and spun our web of dreams. He had just gotten a very good job in the oil fields of western Oklahoma and I had begun working for a small newspaper in Tulsa, trying to decide whether I wanted to pursue my dream of college and a newspaper career. But young love seemed much more important than a college degree so we planned our wedding.

Then, fickle creature that I was, two months later, Jake Campbell walked into the newspaper office and turned my head. Dark, handsome Jake with his ready grin and his knack for making people laugh. Jake was graduating from the University of Tulsa and had a bright future in front of him.

"So, what are you doing stuck in this office, Darcy?" he had asked me. "Why aren't you going to the university here or in Tahlequah? You would be great as a reporter. Now's the time to prepare for tomorrow."

Loyalty to Grant struggled with the excitement and wonder of being near Jake. So, suppressing the guilt I felt over breaking Grant's heart, I married Jake. I regretted the pain I caused Grant, but I had never regretted my decision to share my life with Jake.

Had Grant found somebody else during the years after my marriage? Or maybe there had been a lot of "somebodies" but none that he married. After we broke up, he had quit his job in the oil fields, returned to Levi, and gotten a degree from Northeastern State University in Tahlequah.

Since losing Jake, self-doubt and guilt reared its ugly head. This time, the shoe was on the other foot as far as Grant was concerned. How could I feel that old attraction for him when I was supposed to be a grieving widow? It was a heavy load—one that seemed unbearable at times, one I couldn't talk about to anybody.

Sometime around 3:00 a.m., I slid off into a solid sleep and was dreaming of driving down a strange highway over a river when I became aware the road ahead forked off in two directions. I wasn't sure which fork to take. The meaning of that dream certainly needed no interpretation.

At 6:30, Mom cracked open my bedroom door and called, "Get up, Darcy. We've got some decisions to make and I want to talk to you about some things."

It probably was not permissible to throw a pillow at one's mother. I groaned. "Oh, Mom, I've got a headache and I slept so little last night. Couldn't it wait until eight?"

"No. Get up and take some aspirin. Drink a cup of coffee. We need to be on the road by 8:00 and I want to stop by the donut shop and get some of those cinnamon rolls you like so well."

Experience had taught me there was no arguing with that tone of voice. Then her words finally got through to my foggy brain. *On the road? We need to talk.* What on earth was so vital that it could not wait until later in the day? I slid out of bed and reached for my jeans and a T-shirt. When I stumbled into the kitchen twenty minutes later, Mom was filling a big aluminum thermos with hot coffee.

She glanced at me. "You'd better wear a sweatshirt. It's a little cool this morning."

I grinned. "Yes, Boss. Where are we going, might I ask? I thought we'd covered nearly everything when we talked last night. Has something come up this morning?"

She turned and gave me one of those direct stares that stated plainly now was not the time for discussion. "We're going out to Granny Grace's property. We've got some decisions to make that require plain talk and that's a good place to go to clear our minds of clutter and get away from that telephone!"

"Well, yes, I realize the earthquake stopped me from going out there and you and I both enjoy it, but . . . ."

"Besides," she continued, "you need a little guidance with your life. I'm your mother and it's my responsibility to tell you things you need to know."

Guidance in my life? Had she relapsed a few decades? Why was I being spoken to as if I were a child? I sat with my mouth open and watched her march out the kitchen door.

"We'll take my Toyota," she called over her shoulder.

I usually drove my Escape when we went anywhere together. Apparently, this morning I did not have a choice.

Thirty minutes later, without any further comment or "guidance," Mom pulled her Toyota into the turnaround under the biggest tree on the knoll where my grandparents had lived and she had grown up. The house that overlooked the valley and Ventris River burned down many years ago. Thankfully, it was empty at the time. The land, once owned by Granny Grace's parents, had stayed in our family for four generations. I actually owned it now. It had been Jake's and my dream to build a retirement home here someday had fate not intervened.

Mom handed me the thermos and cinnamon rolls and pulled an old quilt out of the back seat. We walked toward the top of the little hill where the sun was warming the grass. She spread the quilt on the ground and motioned for me to pour the coffee.

She settled down in the sunshine, crossed her legs, and came up with a surprising pronouncement. "I've made a decision."

I poured the coffee, waiting for further information.

"I want to build a new house on this site; that is, if you okay it. We can have it as a retreat and when we feel the need to get out here and think, we won't have to sit on the ground like we are now."

That was a shocker. I had tried to talk her into building a new house for several months but she always responded that she wanted to stay in the old house because she had so many loving memories of my father there.

"But, Mom, I don't understand . . . ."

Then she threw in the clincher: "I've already drawn up a building plan myself. Our house will sit right on top of this hill where we can see for miles in every direction. It will have two bedroom suites—one for each of us—two other big bedrooms, a large office with built-in bookshelves for you, a big kitchen with all new appliances, a four-car garage, a full basement with a storm shelter, four bathrooms, three up and one down—"

"Four bathrooms? Are you serious? Why four bathrooms and why all the spaciousness? This sounds like a mansion instead of a retreat."

Was she well? Maybe she had had some sort of a stroke? This certainly didn't sound like frugal Flora Tucker. But she looked well, happy even. Maybe planning for the future was just what she needed.

She held up one hand. "I know. I know. I'm actually kidding about the four bathrooms. But the point is, Darcy, I've got plenty of money and can afford to build. In fact, I've already called a builder to lay out the location for the basement."

Before I could think of an adequate reply, she gave me a sideways look. "It's time to think about the future, for both of us. I'm only 67. I plan to live for 15 or 20 more years, and there's lots of things I'd like to do, and having a house out here on my mother's old home place is one of those dreams. Your dad and I had once thought to build a home here, just as you and Jake planned to do, but of course that didn't happen."

We sat and thought for a few minutes of the men we had loved. Andy Tucker had been gone for nearly 20 years, but I knew my mother still thought of him every day.

Suddenly she brought up another real shocker of a subject. "And another thing. I believe it's time for you to move on also."

Maybe it was my sleepless night, but I was having trouble keeping up with this conversation. "Are you kicking me out, Mom?"

She snorted. "Of course not. I'm talking about Grant Hendley. Don't think I haven't noticed the way you look at him, and the years obviously have not changed the way he feels about you."

Once again, she gave me no chance to reply, which was a good thing because I seemed to have lost the power to speak.

"When the two of you are together, I can see the attraction. Grant's a good man, a smart man, highly respected in these parts, and I reckon it's time you quit acting like he's somebody you hardly know."

This was a long speech for my mother. Then she added, "Now you look me in the eye, Darcy Campbell, and tell me you don't care about that man."

"But, Mom, Jake hasn't been gone long . . . ."

"I know, Darcy. You feel guilty about still caring for Grant."

Sudden tears stung my eyes and I nodded.

She took my hand. "Look at it this way: You're still young. You've got a lot of good years ahead of you. And if you could ask Jake how he felt about things, do you really think he'd say you should go on just the way you are now, being lonely and missing him all the time? Of course not. He'd say if you had another chance at happiness he'd sure want you to take it."

I squeezed her hand. It was a relief to have her voice all these dilemmas and conflicting thoughts.

"Besides, try to imagine if things were the other way around, and Jake had a chance at a good, smart, hardworking woman who would be a real partner and really love him, wouldn't you want him to grab that happiness?"

I hugged my wise parent. There was no doubt she was right. Once again, Granny Grace's acres and my mother had helped me put things in perspective. One weight had been rolled off my shoulders. I knew without a doubt, whether I told anyone or not, that I still cared deeply for Grant Hendley.

CHAPTER 25

"Pat, Pat, slow down! I can't understand what you are saying."

Mom held the phone's receiver away from her ear but I could hear Pat Harris's excited voice all the way across the room.

Pat must have taken a deep breath and tried to control herself because I could no longer hear her. My mother nodded. "Yes, yes, I see. You think there is something under your garage floor?"

Laying my screwdriver on the cabinet, I went to stand beside her. She and I had been trying to replace cabinet doors since the earthquake and it was a slow process. Screwdrivers and I were not best friends and I had a bloody thumbnail to prove it.

"What is it?" I mouthed the words as Mom looked at me. She shook her head.

"Uh-huh. I see. You want Darcy and me to come? It sounds as if you need a repairman, Pat. Or maybe Jasper could help? Darcy and I don't seem to be much good at fixing things."

Pat's voice rose again and I heard her high-pitched words. "No, no, Flora, I don't need a handyman. Just hurry up and get out here, you and Darcy, too."

Mom replaced the telephone and turned to stare at me. Her eyes were troubled. "I know that earthquakes do strange things, like tornadoes do but I've never heard of a tornado scrambling someone's mind."

"Is that what you think happened to Pat? What did she say?"

My mother sat down at the kitchen table. "She said . . . she said that she hadn't moved her truck out of the garage for a few days until just now. She pulled it out and the tires bumped over a rough place. She got out to look and she thinks there is something under her garage floor."

"Something under . . . that doesn't make sense. Her garage is on ground level, just like her whole house. How could there be anything under it?"

Mom pressed her fingers against her forehead. "She had that garage re-built only about two years ago. She told me she had a brand new floor poured. I remember she was bragging about how the concrete looked so pretty and smooth, not cracked at all."

"So, does she think the earthquake damaged the garage?"

"I guess so."

"Why on earth does she want us to come? What can we do? We can't even take care of repairs on our own house."

"Pat has always run to hysteria when something goes wrong. You've heard that misery loves company? Well, Pat does not suffer in silence. She called Earlene Crowder and Earlene was sympathetic but she didn't offer to come help. All our lives, we were girls together, you know, Darcy, Pat has wanted me to come if she's upset."

I checked the coffee pot. Empty. "She didn't call for you when people suspected Jasper might have something to do with Ben Ventris's death."

"No, that's different. She is very protective of her son."

"I'm tired, Mom, and I'm sure you are. Why don't we just forget about Pat's phone call? Maybe she'll calm down."

Mom went down the hall to the coat closet. "No, I don't think she's going to calm down until I go out there. I don't know what she thinks is under her garage floor, Darcy, but I have the feeling we'd better go. She sounded like she was wound as tight as . . . as . . ."

"As one of her pin curls?"

"Good description. Grab your coat, Darcy. Let's go."

Pat was waiting on the porch when we pulled into her driveway. She hurried down the steps and began talking before she reached my car.

She was twisting her hands inside her apron and when she spoke, her words ran together.

"Oh, Darcy and Flora, thanks so much for coming. I just didn't know what to do. I don't see any damage to my house, but when I was cleaning up some limbs and trash from the yard and I backed out the pickup to haul that stuff down into the woods, well, there it was. With the truck out of the garage I could see there were four big cracks and some little ones in the concrete floor, and when I looked down into the biggest crack . . . ." She paused and shook her head. "There's something under there."

Murphy, the large red hound who lived with Pat and Jasper, thrust his wet nose into my hand.

"There's no need to get upset about it," I told her. "Lots of floors in Ventris County probably have cracks after that quake. Even if it looks bad, I imagine it wouldn't be too hard for a professional finisher to fix."

"Yes, but it's not just the cracks. It's . . . ." Her eyes were as round as Artie's pancakes and her voice dropped to a whisper. "I think there's something under my garage floor."

Mom punched me in the ribs and spoke around her hand. "See what I mean?"

"Miss Pat, there are things under everybody's garage floor. Tree roots reach under the cement after it has been poured. Rocks, maybe even some small animals like moles and gophers could dig under there or—uh . . . ." I looked at Mom. "Trash that was washed under the floor by heavy rains, maybe?"

"I know, but . . ." She circled around her old Ford pickup and headed toward the single garage. "I don't think this is any of those things. I would say it is definitely not trash. No, no." She shook her gray curls.

"Now, Pat," Mom put her arm around her old friend's shoulders, "why would there be anything under your garage floor that's not under every other garage floor in the country?"

"What do you think is under there, Miss Pat?"

She pushed Murphy out of the way and kept walking. "I don't want to say 'cause if it's not what it looks like, you'll think I'm crazy. Come and see for yourself."

Like most homes in Levi, the Harris house was old, probably built in the thirties or before. It was white frame and small with a narrow front porch squarely in the middle. The tiny detached garage had been added after the house was built. I remembered seeing that the garage looked fairly new, at least a lot newer than her house, back in the spring when Mom and I came to talk to Pat about Jasper in connection with Ben Ventris's disappearance. Mom remarked after that visit that it probably cost more to re-build Pat's garage than her old house had cost originally.

There was no automatic opener for Pat's garage door, only two wooden panels that closed in the middle with a sliding bar. Both sides were now propped open by two-by-fours.

The three of us and Murphy stepped inside. Sunlight filtered through, lighting the front of the garage but throwing the back into shadows. I glanced at the ceiling. No light bulb hung there; only a bare socket where the bulb should be.

Pat was right about the cracks; there were several good-sized ones but what caught my attention was the fact that most of the cracks were on the left side of the floor, zigzagging out from what appeared to be a sunken spot in the concrete. That area interested Murphy, too. He immediately plodded over and started nosing and pawing at the cracks.

"My floor is only a couple of years old. The first floor they poured cracked, so they came out and made a whole new floor and rebuilt the garage, too. They said the cement they used at first must not have been any good."

We stepped closer to the damaged area. Mom and I knelt down to look into the biggest crack. I pushed the inquisitive Murphy aside. The morning sun created a glare that nearly blinded me.

I probed the sunken spot with my fingers. "Have you got a flash-light handy, Miss Pat? Some of these cracks are pretty deep and I can't see anything."

Pat stood on tiptoe and reached up to a shelf at the back of the garage. She brought out a big flashlight. As she gave it to me, her hand was shaking. "I couldn't see anything either at first, until I used this light."

Poking around on a garage floor while this near-hysterical woman fluttered above me was not my favorite way to spend the day. Why couldn't she just say what she thought? I leaned closer to the largest crack. "Whatever is in there, if there's anything at all, I don't think it's going to jump out and grab you."

Mom nudged me with her foot. "Darcy."

"Sorry," I muttered. "I shouldn't have said that."

"Well, I'm just not exactly sure what I saw, Darcy. You know what I mean? And I don't want to say what it looked like yet until I get a second opinion. You and Flora know how to keep your mouths shut. 'Cause if it is what I think it is, I sure don't want the whole county to know."

My ever-practical mother spoke. "Now, Pat, don't get yourself all in a lather. Darcy and I are here to help you no matter what you saw. First of all, show us where you were when you saw whatever it is that's upset you so much."

Pat did not move. Wordlessly, she pointed to the spot where I was crouched.

Mom continued, "Now, tell us what it looks like. What color is it? What shape is it? How far down in the crack is it? Can you see most of it?"

Pat closed her eyes. "Oh, Flora, it was glinty. It caught the light and when I looked closer, it sure looked like gold to me. There! I said it."

Gold? The woman had a wild imagination. "Now, Miss Pat, what would gold be doing under your floor? Have you lost a ring? Maybe something fell down in the crack while you were examining it."

Pat laughed. "Are you serious? The only piece of gold I've ever owned is my wedding ring and I put that in a drawer a long time ago. If I had any gold, Darcy Campbell, it'd be in a safety deposit box at the bank."

Was Mom listening? I hoped so. She didn't believe in safety deposit boxes and kept all her valuables in a cedar chest in her room.

Angling the flashlight's beam at the largest crack, I slowly played it across the floor. Aha! Now I saw something. The object Pat was trying to describe was perhaps ten inches down. She was right; it was kind of glinty. It was also dirt-covered. But I needed to see more. I pulled myself up, hoping that my popping knee joint didn't have anything to do with my age, and went out into the yard. I picked up one of the broken twigs from the maple. Murphy ambled out of my way as I came back into the garage.

"I could go get an old rug for your knees," Pat offered.

"No, that's okay. I'll just take a quick poke down here. Mom, can you hold the flashlight for me?"

My mother grabbed the light and I began scratching away some of the dirt from the glinty object that had Pat so unstrung. The thing was hard and seemed to be stuck. Normal, I guessed, since it was under concrete.

"Maybe I could get it out of there if I had a hook. Do you have a wire coat hanger, Miss Pat?"

"Sure." Pat disappeared into the house and came back with the black hanger. I bent it into a longish shape and carefully pushed it into the crack.

"I think I've grabbed onto that shiny thing," I said. I tugged but nothing happened. If it was gold under Pat's garage floor, it seemed to like its location. It refused to budge. I could only glimpse what was holding it down; something long and hard and white. I swallowed. No, I would not even go there. I did not want it to be what it looked to be.

After probing around for a good ten minutes, I pulled to my feet and rubbed my aching back. "It is fastened onto something, Miss Pat. If you are really interested in seeing what it is, I think you are going to have to get somebody out here to further tear up your floor. It's stuck under there and besides that, I think it may be too big to come through the crack."

I did not want to say aloud the reason I feared it would not come through the crack. Pat needed only a nudge to completely go over the brink into full-blown hysteria. I caught her questioning stare. Did she think it might be something a lot more sinister than gold? Was that the reason she was so upset?

She scuffed the floor with the toe of her canvas shoe. "I think I'll just have more concrete poured over it and forget it. As you said, it's probably just a tree root or something. I don't want any trouble at all. Uh-uh."

CHAPTER 26

"Patricia Harris, be sensible. We have got to tell somebody. You can't just cover up that damage and forget it." Mom fidgeted on one end of Pat's gray sofa. I sat on the other end, but I felt as if I would jump straight through the window behind me if anyone said "Boo."

Pat was too nervous to sit. She paced the length of her small living room. She pushed her curls back from her face, twisted her hands together, and made small moaning sounds.

I was afraid she was near collapse. "Miss Pat, please, sit down. Tell me where you keep your coffee or tea. I'll fix something warm for you to drink."

She shook her head. "No, no, thank you kindly, Darcy, but I couldn't swallow a thing." She stopped in front of my mother and shook her finger at her. "Flora Tucker, there's no way under the Lord's heaven that I'm going to tell anybody in law enforcement about anything being buried under my garage floor. Why, if there's something under there that's bad, the first person they would suspect is my Jasper. I won't have it. I won't, I tell you."

I got up, grasped her arm and led her to the floral pink upholstered chair in the room. I gently pushed her down into it then stood in front of her so she couldn't get up and start that infernal pacing again.

"You must get hold of yourself. Nobody is going to arrest Jasper. Why should they? And we are not really sure what's under the garage floor. Maybe it's a . . . maybe it's a . . . well, something entirely innocent."

"Ha! You know better than that, Darcy. And I'm thinking you saw as much as I did. There's more than just a piece of gold under that floor. I've got a real bad feeling about it. And you can't fool me about Jasper. I've seen enough of those detective shows to know that Grant would think Jasper knows about it just because he lives here. Simple as that. And my boy couldn't defend himself. We all know he's a little different, but he wouldn't hurt a fly. And he's never stole anything in his life. Why would he steal something and then bury it? That wouldn't make any sort of sense."

Mom looked thoughtful. "If that shiny thing is gold, it could be part of a batch that was buried way back in the '30s when outlaws robbed banks and then came to the Cookson Hills to hide. If I were you, I'd want to know. You'd be rich, I guess, unless it would have to go back to wherever it came from."

Pat covered her eyes with her apron and began to cry. "I wish I could believe that, Flora. But I don't think that's it. And I wish I'd never seen . . . what I saw. Why did I have to go poking around?"

Mom came to stand beside her. She rubbed her back until Pat quieted and looked up at us through eyes that swam with tears.

"Now, are you ready to talk sensibly?" Mom asked.

Pat nodded.

Mom looked down at her friend. "I didn't get down on my knees and look into that crack so I don't know what you and Darcy think you saw. You're both talking in riddles and I want to know what you're talking about."

"Mom, I hate to say this but it looks like that piece of gold is attached to something under Pat's floor. It's something white and sort of looks like a bone—maybe."

My mother snorted. "Well, of all the silly things! Could it be poor old Murphy hid a bone in there before the men poured the cement on it?"

"Could be. Miss Pat, do you feel calm enough to discuss this with us?"

Pat bobbed her head. "Yes, yes, I'm feeling better. And it could have been Murphy that put it there. He likes to dig. I don't know what

I would've done if you hadn't come, Flora. You're always so down-to-earth."

Mom glanced at me and rolled her eyes. "There are some who would disagree with you. But I believe in facing facts, and not go borrowing trouble. It won't do to jump to conclusions."

"Miss Pat, weren't you here when the garage floor was poured?" I asked.

Pat shook her head. "No, I was over at Goshen Cemetery checking on some vandalism. It was all finished by the time I got back, except for drying, of course. I couldn't use the garage for quite a while so the concrete would set."

Mom walked back to the sofa. "How about Jasper? Was he here?"

"See? Even you, Flora. There you go with Jasper already. I don't think so. Jasper was probably roaming around through the woods. He likes to do that."

"So who poured your floor?" I asked.

"Why, I don't actually know. I phoned the secretary at Gary Worth's construction business. She said she'd send some guys out right away. I don't know who actually came 'cause as I said, I wasn't here."

I opened my purse and took out my cell phone.

Pat grabbed my arm. "What are you doing?"

"I'm going to call Grant. This is what you should have done in the first place, Miss Pat. He has sophisticated equipment to check beneath that cement. That's the only thing to do."

Mom perched on the arm of Pat's chair. "Shouldn't you be calling somebody with a jackhammer, Darcy? If there's nothing bad under there, seems to me you shouldn't be bothering Grant."

Pat drew a long, quavering breath. "No, I guess Darcy's right, Flora. I've always been a law-abiding citizen. If it's a batch of long-buried gold, it might be better to get it all out in the open and not try keeping secrets. Wouldn't work anyhow in this town."

Mom spoke in a soothing tone. "It will be all right, Pat."

Yes, hopefully my mother was right. But I remembered somebody in Dilly's Cafe saying that I should talk to Pat's son. And of course, Jasper had told me he knew a lot of things that others didn't know. He liked to keep secrets. Many people suspected that he murdered Ben Ventris before we found out the identity of the real bad guys.

Sometimes society as a whole looked with suspicion on people who were different. This was unfair and undeserved, but we are an imperfect species. Jasper moved in a realm of woods and animals. He was friends with the owls. Civilized society was locked into a set of established rules. Surely if someone liked God's great outdoors more than he liked people, that little oddity should not cause him to be looked on with suspicion. But buried gold under Pat's floor? No. If Jasper knew about the gold, he would not have buried it. He would have used it to help his mother. Maybe whatever was buried on this place was a remnant of those lawless days of the 1930s. And if there was a bone buried with the gold, perhaps it was some luckless person who got in the way of an outlaw's bullet.

I dialed a familiar number and listened to a familiar voice on the other end of the telephone line. "Grant? This is Darcy. I'm afraid we need you to come to Pat Harris's place."

CHAPTER 27

Grant pulled into Pat's driveway an hour later. We three met him on the porch. He was followed by an older man driving a nearly new white Ford Ranger. Grant introduced him as Paul Hubbard, the owner of a construction company in Oklahoma City. Hubbard was silver-haired and appeared to be about sixty but moved with the agility of a twenty-year-old.

"Paul's been building houses and pouring cement all his working life and he probably knows more about concrete floors than anybody in Oklahoma," Grant said. "He happened to be working on a job here in Levi so I took advantage of that and called him. He'll take a look at the cracks in the garage floor. We may need somebody with a jackhammer before we can do a whole lot. It depends on what Paul finds."

"Since Gary Worth poured the floor in the first place, I thought you might have him come back again. Sort of have him lick his calf over," Mom said.

Grant took off his white Stetson and ran his hand through his hair. He looked and sounded tired. I wondered what, of all the things a law officer faced, was keeping him awake at night.

He turned toward Mom. "And I thought, Miss Flora, that we might should have a new set of eyes look at the situation. If Gary didn't pour that concrete like he should have, do you think he'd be much interested in licking his calf over, as you said?"

Mom looked down and shook her head. It was unlike Grant to speak abruptly, especially to my mother.

I put my arm around her. "Did you get any sleep at all last night?" I asked him.

"Maybe a couple of hours. Too much going on to get a good night's sleep."

Hubbard went straight to Pat and took her hand. "Now, Ms. Harris, Grant said you thought you might have found a gold piece under your garage. That might sound strange, but you turn up some really odd things sometimes when you're digging footings for a foundation. Over the years I've come to understand that there's a lot of things underground that you wouldn't expect."

Pat was still having trouble putting together a coherent sentence. "Yes, but that thing . . . . I mean what else could that shiny thing be but something made out of gold; maybe a bracelet, and if that's the case . . . well, what would a gold bracelet be doing under my garage floor?"

"We thought maybe it was some of the outlaw's gold from the '30s that people keep saying is buried around here," Mom said.

Grant looked at me. "But you thought it was more than that, didn't you?"

"I hope not. I hope I'm wrong."

Hubbard opened his truck and pulled out a black tool kit. "You wouldn't believe how many pieces of jewelry are stuck down in the mud and rocks on this old earth. Sometimes a ring slips off the owner's finger while he or she is swimming. Sometimes a bracelet or watch breaks during a hike or a picnic in the woods and falls into the grass and nobody ever finds it. Why, I remember one case where a wife got mad at her cheating husband while they were walking a nature trail and she took off her two-carat wedding ring and threw it at him." He shrugged. "They never found it. It probably got washed farther away from the original site and someday somebody will be digging and find it and wonder how in the world it got there."

Hubbard stepped into the garage and we all trooped in after him. He stood silently studying the garage floor. He frowned. "The thing that bothers me most is not the fact that a piece of gold may have been buried under your garage, Ms. Harris, but the pattern of cracks in the cement."

"Why is that?" I asked. "The pressure from an earthquake is naturally irregular so wouldn't that lead to more cracks in one area than another?"

He motioned to the southeast corner. "Yes, but not in such a cluster. The pattern of these cracks indicates that the cement was poured a lot thicker in this part of the garage than the rest of the floor. If there was a depression in this corner—which is the only reason I can think of for the floor to be thicker—a savvy contractor would have filled it and leveled the whole thing before bringing in the cement truck."

Hubbard sauntered slowly toward the big crack in the corner of the garage, his eyes searching the floor as he walked. We three women trailed along behind him. Grant went back to his truck and flipped open his cell phone.

Hubbard knelt beside the cracks. "Let's just take a look-see here," he said.

He unsnapped the tool kit and removed a hammer, a big screwdriver, a tiny camera, and a light on a long, flexible handle.

Mom asked, "But if something was in the ground for a long time, wouldn't it change colors? Why are you all thinking it's gold just because it's yellow?"

Hubbard shook his head. "Real gold never changes colors, never tarnishes. Silver and other metals do, but gold doesn't. If it's been in highly acidic soil for years it may get corroded and rough, but gold will never tarnish."

Nobody else said a word. We waited breathlessly for his official pronouncement.

He used the hammer and screwdriver to chip away at the sides of the biggest crack to make room to insert the tiny light. It took him less than two minutes to deliver his verdict. "It looks to be a gold bracelet and a rather unique one at that. There may be some tiny stones in the top, maybe sapphires or rubies."

I grabbed a shelf next to me. My head swam. A bracelet? I didn't want it to be a bracelet.

Pat was still fumbling with words. "You mean . . . was it just there in the ground when the floor was poured, or did it somehow come up—sort of work its way to the top? I mean to the top of the ground underneath the floor and then . . . oh no, that couldn't have happened. Was it . . . ?" She was babbling again. Mom patted her hand and Pat's questions dwindled away.

I bent down beside Paul Hubbard. "Did you find anything else besides a gold bracelet in there? What do you think?" I asked.

Three pairs of eyes were riveted on him. I imagined Mom and Pat were holding their breath as I was. He replaced his tools in the case and closed it with a click that sounded like a gunshot.

Hubbard got to his feet and gave me a hand up. "I think, Ms. Campbell, that it's time for the sheriff to call in the forensic team and the jackhammer man."

CHAPTER 28

I slept very little that night and judging from the light that stayed on in my mother's room, neither did she. At last morning came, one of those blue-sky, crisp-as-a-freshly-ironed shirt days when all of nature seemed to be smiling down on us mere mortals. However, this morning, nature surely would not have been smiling if she was aware of the grim task taking place at Pat Harris's home. By 10 o'clock, Mom and I stood huddled with Pat inside her garage watching a team of experts from Oklahoma City do their morbid but thoroughly professional job.

"A body buried in concrete is a forensic nightmare." The tall, fortyish man who had introduced himself as Chuck Carroll from the state medical examiner's office, shook his head. "By the time you get it out, you've destroyed some of the evidence required for identification."

His partner, Sid Hewgley, stepped forward and peered into the crack. "Yes, but there's usually dental records."

Hewgley turned to Grant. "Sheriff, assuming this woman was buried here when the new floor was poured, what possibilities do we have for her identity? I know about Andrea Worth, of course, but I understand there was a missing persons report filed about the same time on a woman who was traveling through the state with a male friend and also simply disappeared and has never been found."

Grant stood with folded arms, one shoulder leaning against the frame of the garage. "That's right; and there was another report, a woman from Texas, who was supposedly running from an abusive husband and heading toward her sister's house in Oklahoma. She never did get here and nobody ever found her."

These were two that had escaped my notice. But then, I had forgotten a lot of things since Jake's death. Maybe I had known about them at one time but they had slipped my mind.

Pat had been standing wide-eyed, to the side of our little group. She took a deep breath and asked, "But how can you be sure it's a woman? Men sometimes wear bracelets nowadays."

Hewgley turned toward her. "We can be reasonably sure, Ms. Harris, because of the size of the wrist bone we can see down in the crack." Then he spoke to his partner. "Okay, Chuck, let's get our equipment unloaded and get started."

Carroll frowned and spoke to Grant. "So Ms. Harris got Gary Worth to pour the new floor after the old one cracked, then Worth got another small company to pour the concrete? Surely the body was buried when the floor was poured. But, according to Worth, the company he hired has now gone out of business and the owner can't be located?"

Grant nodded. "I talked to Worth yesterday."

"And Ms. Harris was not here when they started on the garage floor and footings." He turned to Pat. "The whole floor was already finished when you got back home?"

Pat nodded.

Chuck Carroll continued, "So if we could find the guy who poured the cement we'd likely have the killer."

"Not necessarily." Grant traced a curving line across the garage floor with the toe of his boot. "Although I'm not an expert, it looks to me like this part where the biggest cracks are might have been taken up after the rest of it was poured, and then a new batch put down in that spot."

He dropped to one knee and examined the area more closely. "And if that's the case, it might explain why this corner of the floor looks a little darker and rougher. It was a slightly different mix."

Carroll shrugged. "I suppose that's possible. If the murderer knew about the floor replacement, and knew that Ms. Harris was out of pocket, he waited until the first concrete guys left, then brought the body in and reworked this corner."

Sid Hewgley had been examining the cracks and attempting to draw a computerized outline of the body. "The bone structure looks like this is definitely a woman. The body is lying slightly on its side but she was probably about 5 feet 4 inches tall."

Mom blinked. "You mean you can tell all that with that little gadget—what do you call it?"

"A spectrograph," Hewgley explained. "It's sort of like an X-ray. But what we can see with it probably won't help us identify her. That will have to wait until we get her out."

He used a big piece of chalk to make an oval on the floor over the approximate location of the victim.

Mom was hot on the trail of this one. "So since this person has been here since the floor was poured, how are you going to be able to tell who she was? How will you be able to identify her?"

"Maybe I know of a way," I said. I had learned quite a bit about forensics through my crime reporting, and my mother was right. Identifying a body after a couple of years, particularly if further damage was done when the cement floor was broken up, would not be an easy task, and we would have to wait for DNA results.

The first person I thought of was Andrea Worth, but at the same time, I was sincerely hoping it was not. Was Sophie's two-year wait for answers about to come to an end?

Taking Mom's arm, I led her out of the garage. A flock of wild geese flew over, heading south. They would probably stop to rest at the river before flying on to warmer climes. A few tenacious maple leaves, hanging onto the tree until the last moment, let go and fluttered down around us. A blue jay scolded us from his perch in an oak tree. On the surface, nature went about its peaceful business. But a few feet away, human emotions surged.

Mom sighed. "It's a beautiful day. Far too pretty for that painful thing going on inside the garage."

"Yes, you're right. Mom, didn't Sophie tell you that Andrea was fond of bracelets and had some made by a custom designer there in Amarillo?"

She looked thoughtful. "Yes, I believe she did."

"Then maybe Sophie would remember if Andrea had a bracelet like this one we've found."

Tears clouded my mother's dark eyes. "Oh, Darcy, I do hope that isn't Andrea under all that cement. Poor, poor Sophie."

"She will have to know, one way or the other. I don't want to call her until I'm sure, and even then, I don't want to inform her of what we've found with just a phone call. She's going to need someone with her."

Mom nodded agreement and we went back inside the garage.

I walked over to Carroll. "So getting her out is going to take several hours of painstaking work, and maybe several days more of lab tests by the medical examiner."

Carroll nodded. "Not much else to do."

"I have an idea," I told them. "If it works, it'll provide much faster on-the-site results. Her final identification may not be confirmed until the medical examiner does his job, but I can think of a way that will give us a foot up in the right direction."

All action stopped. Grant stepped to my side. He well knew that my background gave me a little insight the others might not have. "What are you thinking about, Darcy?"

"The bracelet," I explained. "Sophie Williams told Mom that her daughter had several pieces of jewelry custom made by a designer in Amarillo. From what your probe has discovered, this bracelet appears to be unique. If we can get a good look at it, and if it isn't Andrea's bracelet, why then . . . ." I prayed to the good Lord that it wasn't Andrea's, but if not, the fact remained that some other poor soul rested under Pat's floor. "Why then, we'll know it's somebody else under there. And if it appears to be one of those pieces made by that jeweler, then we'd be pretty close to having a positive identification."

My mother whispered, "May the Lord have mercy on her, whoever she is."

"And mercy on her family," Pat added.

"Mom, do you think you'd remember the name of the jeweler that Sophie mentioned if you heard it again?"

She thought for a few seconds. "Yes, I think I would if I heard it again. It was a different name: Alonzo's, Aladdin's, something that started with an A like Amarillo."

"First, we'd need to get a picture of that bracelet, Grant, then I can call the jeweler in Amarillo. If he recognizes it as one of his own creations that he made for Andrea, it would be close to proof positive, wouldn't it? Maybe not forensic proof, but surely something pretty strong."

Chuck Carroll pulled a pad out of his pocket and started sketching. Then he handed it to me. "This is roughly how it appears. I can't see the underside, of course, but I think the top part is some sort of oval faceplate with edging around the oval and five small stones—maybe rubies, set in some kind of diagonal pattern. I'll poke around down in there and get the best photo possible under the circumstances."

I studied the sketch. "This ought to be enough for me to use when I talk to the jeweler. It's unusual enough that he will probably recognize it from my description, if it really is Andrea's."

Hopefully, the wonder of technology via my Internet search button on my cell phone would give us an answer. I started scrolling down the list of jewelers in Amarillo.

"That's it," Mom interrupted. "Adolpho. I remember now."

I punched in the listed number. A brusque, guttural voice answered. I gave him my name. "I have recently seen a beautiful bracelet, a gold bracelet that I greatly admire," I told him. I did not think it was necessary to tell him where I had seen it. "A friend told me that it came from your shop; in fact, that you had custom made it for a woman by the name of Andrea Worth. Or, you might know her by her maiden name, Williams. I'm hoping you could make one for me just like it. If I describe it to you, do you think you would remember it?"

"But of course. I keep records on all my custom-made jewelry. What did the bracelet look like?"

"It is maybe half an inch wide, yellow gold, and the faceplate is edged with rubies in a diagonal pattern."

"Hmm. It does sound lovely. But then, all my pieces are. And you say her last name was Williams or Worth? Let me check my files."

Adolpho presumably walked to his computer and started pressing keys. Two minutes later, he was back with me.

"I found the item you described. I also took a picture of it after it was finished. And I remember the lady who bought it now. Her first name is Andrea but her last name is Mott. She had drawn the pattern herself and knew exactly what she wanted on it. She said it was to be a gift from her husband, Tom Mott."

With a sinking feeling, I thanked Adolpho and closed my phone. The forensic team would make the final confirmation but this information was all I needed. We had indeed found Andrea Worth. Now if we could just find her murderer.

Mom and Pat, Sid Hewgley, Chuck Carroll, and Grant were all silently staring at me.

"Sounds like the bracelet is Andrea's."

Pat moaned. "Oh, no."

Mom just shook her head.

Carroll spoke quietly, "We'll have to do the forensic work anyway."

"What should I do about Sophie, Grant?" I asked.

"I can't officially notify Andrea's mother until we are finished with the lab work. This doesn't mean that you have to wait on that before you talk to her, Darcy."

"Mom? What should I do?"

My mother reached into her pocket for a tissue. She wiped her eyes and blew her nose. "The police will notify the Amarillo police and someone will go to Sophie's home or her shop. But, if it were me, I'd want to know right away. I think Sophie will want to be here in Levi."

"But just a phone call, Mom. How sad that would be! And how heartless. She needs to be told gently by someone who can put their arms around her. She needs family."

An idea came to me. I still had Charlene's phone number in my cell phone. Charlene had seemed different, a little more likable that last night in Amarillo. I thought that her rough exterior might be covering some actual softer feelings. I would give her a call and ask her to go to her aunt in person and tell her the sad news. I would also ask her if she would drive to Levi with Sophie. I didn't think it would be safe for Sophie to drive that long distance alone.

I checked my cell phone and punched in Charlene's number.

A few minutes later, I broke the connection and slipped the phone back into my purse. Charlene had sounded genuinely sad. She had not hesitated to say she would go to Sophie right away and yes, she would certainly come to Levi with her.

One more phone call was necessary but that would wait until I got home. In my old address book was the number for Max Sutton at the *Dallas Morning News*. I would bet that Max was still there in his office, stubby pencil behind his ear, making sure that all was ready for the next edition. I needed some information and Max was a source of unending facts and figures.

CHAPTER 29

Shuffling best describes the way Mom came into the kitchen the next morning. One look at her haggard face told me her night had been as long and painful as mine.

"Did you sleep at all?" I asked.

She shook her head and answered, "Not much."

Opening the cabinet door, she reached for a mug. "I'm glad you have coffee ready, Darcy. For the first time in my life, I think I'd put a dollop of whiskey in my cup this morning if we had any in the house."

For my mother, the teetotaler, this was quite a statement. I put my arm around her. "We'll just have to hang in there for a while longer. We have found Andrea and we know that she didn't run away, but we don't know who killed her. Maybe you'd like to take a little trip when this is all over?"

She shook her head. "It'll never be over for poor Sophie and it isn't over yet for any of us."

We had stayed with Pat the previous evening until the forensic team finally got the dead girl's body out of her concrete grave and loaded into the white van.

"I don't think I've ever spent a more horrible day than yesterday," I said. It was not only horrible, it was long. We hadn't left Pat's until 9 o'clock.

I put a couple of place mats on the table for our coffee mugs. "You know, if we hadn't had those two quakes, that grave beneath Pat's garage might never have been discovered."

"The Lord moves in wondrous ways," Mom quoted. "I had wondered why we here in Oklahoma suffered those two quakes but maybe that's why—so that pitiful body could be uncovered."

The steaming mug felt good to my cold hands. "Hmm. Probably the first quake weakened the floor of Pat's garage and the second quake just finished it off. Do you really think the reason for the quakes was so that grave would be found?"

"There's a reason for everything," Mom said.

My mother believed that behind every physical happening lay a spiritual meaning. In other words, we couldn't see the spiritual side of things; we could only see the results of the spiritual.

"You've told me that all my life. I wish, though, that Pat had agreed to come home with us last night. If this grisly find was hard on us, I can't imagine how it must have affected Pat."

But Pat hadn't budged. "No," she had declared, "this is my home and I'll stay here like I've done for 40 years."

Then Pat had gotten a little teary-eyed. "But I don't think I'll ever sleep again without having this nightmare."

She echoed my feelings.

"I keep thinking about her and Jasper," Mom said. "They're out there in that little house all by themselves with no near neighbors. You know Pat and her nerves. I don't imagine she went to bed at all."

"Maybe it was best that she stayed at home. Jasper has the habit of popping up unexpectedly and I'm betting he was close enough to see everything that was happening yesterday. As soon as he knew everybody had gone, he probably came home. There's no telling how he reacted to all that. I think Jasper is why Pat felt like she needed to stay there."

Mom picked up her mug and went over to stare out of the kitchen window. "Do you reckon Gary Worth is the one who killed Andrea?"

"I don't think there are a lot of possibilities. Several people would benefit from Andrea's death. Of course, Gary would inherit her wealth."

"But why would he do that? If he didn't want to live with her, he could have just gotten a divorce."

A spot over my right eyebrow was beginning to ache. "Law enforcement always looks at close family members first as possible suspects in a murder. When a woman is killed, they look at her husband or boyfriend. Sometimes it's a crime of passion, sometimes it's a planned murder; premeditated."

"I called an old friend in Dallas last night after we got home, Mom," I said.

"You did? I was so tired, I took a couple of aspirin, ate a tiny slice of that apple pie left in the refrigerator, and soaked in a hot tub. Almost fell asleep in there. And even after all that, I didn't rest."

I hadn't wanted the small slice of pie last night. I had showered, slipped into my flannel pajamas, and dialed Max Sutton.

"Well, what did your old friend say, Darcy?"

"He's looking up some information for me, Mom."

"About Andrea?"

"Actually, about Gary Worth."

Once again I could hear again Max's nasal twang when he answered the phone. He had been in Texas twenty years but anyone could tell he was from New Jersey the second he started to speak.

It brought back memories to hear him say, "Newsroom. This is Sutton."

"Hello, Maxie. This is Darcy Campbell."

"Will wonders never cease? Is it true what I've been hearing about you? I thought you went to Oklahoma to have some peace and quiet, but everything I've heard is unbelievable! You got involved with some Chicago crooks?"

"I'm afraid most of what you've heard is true. And you won't believe what I'm in the middle of now."

It took five minutes to explain what was going on in Levi and another ten to answer his questions. He ended with, "So how can I help?"

"What I need from you, Maxie, is some of that insider information newspaper guys always have; not hard facts that you can publish, but rumors, gossip, and anything else you can tell me about Gary Worth."

"Let me write that down." I pictured him scribbling on his notepad. "Yeah. I remember that name but it has been a while. Let me do some checking; there're several people here who are oracles, know what I mean? They hear something; they don't forget. I'll check through some old files, too. I remember that our paper ran a couple of stories on that girl that vanished from Levi a couple of years ago. Gary was her husband?"

"Right, Maxie. If you can get back to me soon, I'd appreciate it."

Then after that phone call, I had fallen into bed, only to have horrible dreams.

I got up and went to the cabinet. I needed a couple of aspirins. Maybe they and the coffee would dispel the fog that had settled over my brain. I must have spent at least three hours last night in what passed for sleep, wrestling with faceless killers. I needed to be in top form for the mission I had planned for today, if I could possibly get away by myself. But after the ordeal at Pat's last night, top form seemed like a vain hope. I felt plain awful.

But, feeling awful or in fine fettle, I was determined, somehow, before the day ended, to find that shortcut to Gary Worth's ranch.

And I was worried about my mother. She was a lifelong friend of Pat's and we both had gotten to know and like Sophie. Mom was really emotionally involved in this murder. She couldn't even sit in one place for long this morning. Nerves kept her moving. If she would put her considerable insight into trying to resolve this case, she might feel she was helping her friends and in the process, help herself cope.

"So Max is going to find out all he can about Gary?" Mom asked. "Oh, Darcy, what a tangle this is. Old timers would say that it's a coil. I think Andrea might have gotten in the way of Gary or somebody else who thought she was too dangerous to live."

"Those are my thoughts exactly. One thing leads to another and trouble just keeps building. Think about all the lives affected by the death of Andrea Worth. Come and sit down," I said, patting the table. "I need your expertise."

Her lips twitched in a small smile but she brought her coffee and sat across from me. "I don't know about the expertise but I'd sure like to see the murderer brought to justice."

I rolled the hem of the place mat between my fingers and thought out loud. "Okay. Let's just assume that Gary is the murderer. Did he kill her at the ranch or did he kill her somewhere else?"

"Hmm. Well, didn't the reports say that the officials who searched his ranch found no blood nor any kind of evidence of a struggle or foul play?" she mused.

"Yes. That's what they said. And security cameras at the ranch didn't show anybody coming or going."

"I think if he had killed her there at home, something would have come to light. Was anybody else in the house the day she was supposed to have disappeared?"

"The guard on duty . . . ."

"I wonder what Gary was afraid of, to have a guard and security cameras here in Ventris County?" she interrupted. "Good night! This isn't Chicago."

"That's a good question, Mom. But he did have a guard and that gentleman swore that he came up to Gary's truck and talked to him just before he left for work and there was nobody else inside the truck at that time."

"The cleaning lady came about eight o'clock that morning and Andrea was gone and her bed had not been slept in. I remember reading that in the newspaper article." Mom turned her coffee mug round and round. "Maybe Andrea ran away. Maybe some vagrant found her and killed her after she left her home."

"Possibility, I guess."

I went to the catch-all drawer under the telephone and pulled out a small notepad and pencil. Sitting down again, I turned to Mom. "Okay, I'm going to jot down some things as we think about them."

"First thing, Andrea disappeared without a trace. Why? Did she know something that made her too dangerous to live?"

"Good question, Darcy," Mom said. "But what could she have known?"

"We'll find out when the murderer is brought to justice. And he will be brought to justice. I'm sure of it."

"Is it a 'he,' Darcy? Remember that Charlene was not fond of her cousin."

"I don't think she really hated her, Mom. She was spiteful but she seemed genuinely dismayed when I called her."

"Maybe more than one person was involved in her murder, Darcy."

Good thought. I jotted that down with a question mark after it.

"Ugh. That coffee is cold," Mom said. "Tom Mott, Darcy. List him as a suspect. He's supposed to have an alibi but who knows for sure?"

"Right. And, then, of course, Jasper Harris."

"Jasper? Oh, no, Darcy. I can't picture Jasper as being violent."

"I can't either, unless he lost his temper. Remember back in the spring when Tom Bill Monroney insinuated that Pat had taken some money belonging to the cemetery fund? Jasper almost flattened him. Scared Tom Bill so bad that he left town for a while."

"Okay," Mom said slowly. "List Jasper."

"Remember that Andrea turned up in Pat's garage. It would have been easy for him to bury her while his mother was away from home."

"Or, like I said, it could have been a vagrant," Mom said. "Maybe it was somebody who found her away from her house and thought she had money on her."

"She left without her purse, Mom. Remember?"

My mother left her cold coffee on the table and walked back to the window. "Oh, I don't know. The whole thing boggles my mind. I just feel sorry for Sophie."

She swiped at a foggy spot on the window. "We were really early birds this morning, Darcy. In fact, the birds are just now coming to their feeders."

I joined her at the window. The sun had come up as we talked and the day was turning out to be beautiful. It seemed more like spring than autumn. Somehow, it was comforting to know that nature kept to its eternal cycle, no matter what the whims or sins of mankind.

"I'm glad Sophie called us when she and Charlene got to Levi last night," Mom said.

"I wish they had stayed the night here or at least agreed to come for breakfast this morning, but I'm sure she needs some time alone. She was going to go talk to Grant as soon as his office opened."

The doorbell shrilled. "It's awfully early for company," I said, looking at Mom.

Mom hurried to the front room. "Maybe that's Sophie now."

The front door squeaked as she opened it. I had planned to oil it for a month. Then I heard Mom say, "Well, goodness! Jackson Conner! Come in. You're just in time for breakfast."

I set another placemat on the table and filled another mug with coffee.

Jackson was smiling as he followed Mom into the kitchen. "Darcy, I have some information for you. I thought I'd come and tell you in person rather than phoning."

"Great. Would you like toast with that coffee?"

"No, thanks. Just coffee is fine."

My mother pointed to a vacant chair. "Now Jackson, you don't have to have an excuse for dropping in but since you did, I've got some news for you, too, if you haven't heard."

The smile disappeared from the lawyer's face. "If you're talking about the body found under Pat Harris's garage, yes. I do know about that. But I haven't heard if there has been a positive identification."

There was no reason to tell Jackson about my phone call to Adolpho's. He might have a lawyer's reaction and say I should have let Grant do that. But I was grateful for the diversion of his visit because it was obviously doing my mother an enormous amount of good.

She placed a bowl of sugar and a small pitcher of half 'n' half on the table. How did she know this man required these things for his coffee? And Flora Tucker, thoughtful sleuth, appeared flushed. Her eyes sparkled and she looked at Jackson Conner like he was a cool drink of water on a hot summer day. Was there something about these two that I should know?

The kitchen chair creaked as he settled comfortably into it. His cherry pipe aroma had come into the house with him. To see this man sitting at our table filled a vacancy that I hadn't realized existed. I could only surmise Mom felt the same way I did.

"Mighty fine coffee, Flora," he said. "A good way to start the day."

It was hard not to just blurt out the question I was burning to ask. He said something about information. I couldn't be rude and say, "What information?" but I did wish he'd tell us the reason for his early morning visit. I felt pretty sure it was not entirely for a cup of Mom's coffee.

After draining his mug of its contents, he fished in his jacket pocket. "You remember showing me that picture of a knife you found out at Spirit Leap, Darcy?"

Mom frowned at me. I had not planned to tell her about my visit to the lawyer. I nodded.

"And I told you that it looked familiar but I couldn't recall why or where I had seen it before."

"Yes, I remember our conversation."

"It seemed to me that at one time I had a knife similar to that. So I rummaged through my dresser drawer and finally through my junk drawer and Eureka! Success!"

He brought out a duplicate of the knife I had found at Spirit Leap and placed it on the kitchen table.

"Great! That's wonderful, Mr. Conner. Does your knife still have the lettering intact?"

"Indeed it does." He scooted it across the table to me.

Turning it over, I read aloud, "Cobblestone Homes. Hmm. It doesn't ring a bell."

Mom leaned over my shoulder and studied it. "It is jiggling my memory but I can't quite put my finger on why."

Jackson nodded. "Those were promotional knives Gary Worth handed out when he started a construction business a few years ago.

It didn't do so well. But then a while later he began another business which is the one he runs now. From all I hear, it is doing well and so is Gary."

I handed the knife back to Jackson Conner. "So if Gary used this as a promotional item for a business, he handed out bunches of them."

Jackson nodded. "Probably hundreds."

"So we don't know who has them and who doesn't."

He tapped the knife with his finger. "Right. We don't know how many are still in use and how many are forgotten in a junk drawer as mine was."

Mom shuddered. "It looks evil to me. I don't even want to touch it."

"Inanimate objects are not evil, Mom. Knives, guns, whatever. People can use them for good or for evil. You know that Dad always carried a knife and kept a gun in the house, too."

"Oh, I know, Darcy, but I've just never liked guns and maybe this knife seems evil 'cause it's like the one you found out at Spirit Leap."

Jackson Conner smiled. "I'd better be getting along to my office. Thanks for the coffee. Try to get your minds on some pleasant things, the both of you. You can depend on those forensic experts to do an excellent job and Darcy, you let Grant handle this investigation, you hear? You ladies have a day as wonderful as the two of you."

My, my. Was Jackson Conner Irish? He certainly sounded like he had kissed the Blarney stone. I didn't notice until he had driven away that he left his knife on my mother's kitchen table.

Chapter 30

Jackson Conner had not been gone long when I heard a car pull into our driveway. I looked out to see Charlene's little Crossfire in the driveway and Sophie and Charlene Williams walking up to the front porch.

"Sophie's here," I called to Mom. I opened the door. Mom was right behind me and folded Sophie into a warm hug. Sophie's eyes were red from crying and she hadn't taken time to apply any makeup.

Charlene patted her aunt on the back.

"Oh, Flora, Darcy, I've just come from your sheriff's office. They think the preliminary tests show that was Andrea out at Mrs. Harris's place. I just knew it was, ever since you called Charlene yesterday, Darcy."

She blew her nose on a wadded up tissue she carried.

"Come into the kitchen, both of you," Mom said. "Charlene, I am so glad you came with Sophie."

Sophie sniffled. "She has been a real help."

I led them toward the warmth of the kitchen. "Please come in and sit down. Would you both like some coffee? Have you had breakfast?"

Sophie shook her head. "I couldn't eat anything, but a cup of coffee would be nice. I've brought something I think everybody should know about."

"I had a roll earlier," Charlene said, "but thanks."

Sophie carried a manila folder under her arm that I had not noticed until we stepped into the brightly lit kitchen. She collapsed into the chair vacated by Jackson Conner and Charlene sat next to her. Sophie handed me the folder.

Sophie talked while I pulled some documents from the folder.

"Andrea brought these papers to me about a year before she and Gary were married. I'm not even sure if she knew him then. I had already made a will leaving everything I own to her in the event of my death. She said she was going to make one just like it, giving all her property to me, since the two of us were the only ones left in our immediate family. But if she ever made such a will I never saw it and apparently neither did anybody else. Some of that stuff she inherited from her grandmother and some came in a divorce settlement from Tom. Then some she acquired when she worked in New York, before marrying Tom, but I actually can't find out what happened to all those assets."

The pages in the folder detailed stocks, bonds, annuities, and a New York bank account. These had been in Andrea's name only; not Andrea's and Tom's, and not in Andrea's and Gary's. Andrea Worth had been a wealthy woman.

I looked up from scanning the pages. "So you don't have any idea what happened to all these assets?"

Sophie shook her head. "Not those, no. Of course, I do know that the Inglenook is still in Andrea's name. It isn't listed there because her grandmother stipulated it would always remain in the direct lineage of her family."

"All I can think of to say is Wow," I whispered. "Andrea left all that to come to Ventris County and live with Gary? It must have been love."

Sophie lifted her shoulders. "Or something like that."

Mom read the pages over my shoulder. "This falls right in line with the things we were talking about earlier, doesn't it, Darcy?"

It did indeed, and provided a mighty powerful motive for Andrea's husband to do away with her.

Suddenly Sophie put down her coffee mug. "I want to go and see the place where they found her—where they found my girl."

"Now, Aunt Sophie, we've talked about that," Charlene said in a pleading tone.

Mom's voice was soft. "Oh now, Sophie, I don't know what good it would do and it would just make you feel worse."

Sophie pushed her hair back from her forehead and closed her eyes. "I don't think I could possibly feel any worse. If you and Darcy would take us over to Pat Harris's place, I'd really appreciate it. I don't know if I could find the Harris house by myself, and I'd hate to walk in on poor Pat since I'm a stranger to her."

There it was—a way for me to get off by myself this morning and do some investigating on my own. But what plausible reason could I give for not going with them?

"Mom, you go and show them the way. I think Charlene should go too as a support for Sophie. I've got to do a few things myself; I have never gotten a really good start on that book I'm supposed to be writing. This might be a good time to do that."

None of this was a lie. It was all true. I just didn't say that the few things I had to do involved going the back way to the Worth ranch if, by chance, Gary was at his construction company or otherwise occupied away from home.

My mother arched an eyebrow and looked at me. "It's funny to me, Darcy, that you'd have an itch to work on that book just this minute. Do you have something up your sleeve?"

She really did know me well. "Mom, I'm just doing what you've always preached to me: 'don't put off 'til tomorrow what you can do today.'"

It was with a great sense of relief that I saw the three women climb into my mother's Toyota and head down the road on their way to Pat Harris's house.

The first phone call I made was to Grant. I got straight to the point. "So, have you arrested anyone yet for Andrea Worth's murder?"

"Arrested who, Darcy?"

I was glad Grant couldn't see me stomp my foot. This man could exasperate a stone statue. "Gary Worth comes to mind."

Grant sighed. "First we need proof. I agree that a lot of circumstantial evidence points to Gary. But he has a pretty good alibi in the words of his night watchman and also the film from his surveillance camera. It may take a while, but I guarantee you, we'll find who murdered Andrea Worth. We have some substantial leads. Let me tell you, Darcy, that the person who killed Andrea is probably feeling a lot of pressure right about now. He's scared and desperate and such a person as that is mighty dangerous. So let me handle this. Okay?"

"Okay," I mumbled.

As I hung up the phone, I came to one conclusion: the wheels of justice grind mighty slowly. I'd see if I could speed them up a bit.

My next call was to my cousin Zack Crowder. He drove a truck for Gary occasionally, he said. Surely he would know whether his boss was home. I sincerely hoped he wasn't.

CHAPTER 31

Jethro wound around my legs as if he were trying to tell me something so I checked his food dish. "You've got plenty to eat, pampered cat. Do you want a bite of frozen yogurt?"

He followed me to the freezer. I pulled out the vanilla dessert, scooped up a hefty spoonful and dropped it in his dish. "Eat up."

He needed no encouragement. He tucked his tail around his legs, crouched over this yummy treat and dug in.

Zack had told me that Gary would be out of town for a few days on a cattle-buying trip. That, coupled with the fact that my mother did not know of my intentions made this the perfect time to take a little hike through the woods in the direction of Gary Worth's ranch.

"Now I'm going to do what I've been wanting to do," I told Jethro. He ignored me. "I'm going to do my best to find that shortcut to the Worth ranch. The weather is cooperating and it's a long time 'til night and, best of all, Gary isn't going to be home. So I should be okay."

Thank goodness Mom was occupied with Sophie and Charlene. She would raise a fuss about my trip or want to go with me. Neither of which was going to happen.

I went into the front room, slid open the bookcase drawer containing Dad's old pistol, and stuck it in my purse. This time I was going to be prepared in case I got into trouble. Would the gun be lethal if used on a panther? Hopefully, I wouldn't have reason to find out, but if one of those beautiful but dangerous cats threatened me, maybe the noise of a gunshot would scare it away.

As I was about to go out of the door, I noticed Jackson Conner's pocketknife. It still lay on the table where he left it. If I had to wade through tangles of briers or sumac, the blade on that knife might be very useful.

The knife fit nicely into a small zippered compartment inside the lining of my purse and, feeling a bit like a pioneer woman about to brave the wilderness, I left the house and climbed into my Ford Escape.

The countryside of Ventris County closed around me once I turned off the road that led to Granny Grace's acres and inched along the dim wagon ruts. A big gray limestone rock marked where I had parked my car the day of the thunderstorm. A faint and little traveled path led away from the rock through a dense growth of scrub oak, black jack, and sassafras. I slung my purse over my shoulder, grabbed the flashlight from the glove compartment, and slid out onto a carpet of dead brown leaves.

What did I think I'd find at the Worth ranch? I didn't actually know but sometimes putting myself in the place of somebody else helps me see things more clearly. From all accounts, Andrea's home was the last place she had been seen. Something might turn up; I might have some insight as to how Gary had caused Andrea to vanish if indeed Gary was the culprit.

Every clue that came to light pointed in that direction. If he was responsible for ending the life of Sophie's daughter, I wanted no better reward than to see him behind bars.

Full sunlight on the autumn leaves made the trail show up better than the last time I had tried to follow it.

The trees around me, the silence of the forest, and the fresh scent of damp leaves welcomed me. Did Cherokee people use this path a long time ago? Maybe Gary's ranch had been built on what was once a Cherokee settlement, more than 150 years ago. I remembered hearing that there were springs of water that fed a crystal-clear creek running through his pastures. Gary Worth had chosen well; his place was prime land for raising cattle.

The cawing of a crow broke the stillness as I trudged along, my eyes to the ground so that I wouldn't miss the indistinct track. At times, the limbs of the bushes and trees met overhead, creating a false sense of twilight. I had to duck down under this woodsy canopy. A four-wheeler could navigate this path, or a horse if the rider bent down low over the saddle horn. But in no way could a car, no matter how compact, get through.

The trees drew back from the trail now so maybe I was nearing Gary's pasture. I glanced up to see if a building were in sight. Gary Worth, his arms folded across his chest, his legs straddling my path stood six feet away, staring at me.

His lips drew back in a smile completely devoid of mirth. "Well, well, if it isn't little Darcy. The intrepid reporter hot on the trail for a news story. And this time she's really on the trail. That's a joke. Get it, Darcy?"

A surprised yelp escaped me before I clamped my lips shut. This man was supposed to be gone from home. How had he known that I would be here? Did he regularly patrol this back way to his ranch? Judging from his face and voice, he was no happier to see me than I was to see him. If I needed any proof that appearances can be deceiving, it came in the form of Gary Worth. How could someone who was so good to look at be such an evil person?

Sometimes subterfuge comes in handy. This was one of those times.

My mouth suddenly felt dry. I cleared my throat. "Gary! Am I glad to see you! I was out in the woods, um, looking for mushrooms and I'm afraid I got lost. If you'll just point the way back to the road, I'll be going. I sure didn't mean to trespass on your land, if that's what I'm doing."

He shook his head and started walking toward me. If I had ever seen hatred in someone's eyes, it glittered in the green eyes of Andrea's husband. "No, I don't think so, Darcy. You're too nosy, too stubborn. I can't have you messing up things now."

I turned and ran. And bounced off the broad chest of my cousin Zack Crowder. The relief that washed through me left me weak. I grasped his arm.

"Zack! Am I glad to see you! Zack, this guy . . ." I turned and pointed at Gary who stood much too close, "this guy threatened me. I'm afraid he knows what happened to Andrea."

My babbling would have put Pat Harris to shame but I didn't care. I just wanted Zack to get me far away from Gary Worth, immediately if not before.

But Zack was not behaving as I wanted him to behave. He stood stock still, gazing down at me and slowly shaking his head.

"I'm afraid that I'm not here to rescue you, Cousin Darcy."

I rubbed both hands over my eyes. What was he saying? Zack didn't even look the same. I had never seen his face set in those lines and he kept shaking his head.

Behind me, Gary laughed. That low, throaty noise sent chills racing down my backbone.

"Zack, what are you talking about? Don't you know that this man," I jabbed a thumb toward Gary, "this guy probably killed Andrea? Didn't you hear about her body being found at Pat Harris's? He's evil, Zack. Don't you know that? What's wrong with you?"

"Sure, I knew that Andrea had been found. That loudmouth Pat phoned Mom, and Mom likes to tell everybody just how much she knows. She didn't know about me and Gary though. She'd never have guessed that I helped Gary get Andrea off the ranch and put her body under that floor. And, she's not going to know, Darcy. By the time your wonderful Grant Hendley finds you, everybody is going to believe that poor old Jasper Harris killed Andrea and you, too."

This nightmare was far too real. When would I wake up? I felt as if I were in a different dimension where people looked sane but were actually as crazy as bedbugs. My purse was in front of me, slung there when I bumped into Zack. Gary was behind me. Slowly, I eased open the clasp and reached for my dad's gun.

But Zack saw the movement. "No, you don't, Cousin." He grabbed my purse off my shoulder and tossed it to Gary.

"That takes care of your cell phone and whatever else you might have had in there. Turn around, Darcy."

Gary rummaged through my purse and came out with Dad's gun. He pointed it at me. "Lookee here. The little lady is armed."

My stomach knotted.

"Put that thing down," Zack snapped. "We're not quite ready for that yet. Her purse will be useful when we put some evidence on Jasper."

For the first time I noticed that Zack had a length of rope. He grabbed my shoulders and spun me so that I faced Gary. I felt the rope go around my wrists behind my back. I shook my head to clear it. This was happening too fast. This hallucination felt real. Surely it must be a bad dream. Zack, my cousin, however how many times removed, but still a relative. And his mother Earlene. Why, she and Mom visited sometimes and Earlene took an active role in the upkeep of Goshen Cemetery just as Mom did. When had Earlene's son begun to change?

"Zack," I said, "think about what you're doing. Think about your parents. This is not like you. Nobody in the family has ever been mixed up with murder. It's not too late. If you turn Gary in to Grant, you'll be a hero."

"Shut up, Darcy." He gave the rope around my wrists a yank.

Zack had made the mistake of stepping too close to me while he was tying my hands. I twisted out of his grasp. Lowering my head, I rammed it as hard as I could into his stomach.

"Ow! You'll be sorry for that, Darcy. I'll make sure you are good and sorry." A thousand stars exploded somewhere behind my eyes and thick blackness closed in around me.

CHAPTER 32

I awoke to the sound of a beating drum. Funny; it was beating with the same rhythm as my heart; a pulsating beat that hurt. In fact, the top of my head felt as if it would explode. I tried to open my eyes but that only increased the pain. Gary or Zack must have hit me on the head with something pretty hard. I lay very still until the pounding lessened. Then, when the noise of blood pulsating in my ears subsided, I could hear voices: Gary's and Zack's voices.

Where was I? I cautiously wiggled my fingers and tried to move my feet. They were tied, too. I seemed to be lying on something scratchy. I could feel it through my shirt and against my ankles where my jeans had ridden up.

And then I smelled hay. I opened my eyes, just a slit, so that my captors wouldn't know that I had regained consciousness. The building where I lay was big and shadowy. It looked like a barn. Had they put me in one of Gary's barns? Was I still at the Worth ranch?

The two men sat on stools or kegs near a door. It was a tall, wide door, big enough for a tractor and trailer loaded with hay to get through. The door looked to be on tracks and it was pushed back about two feet, wide enough to let in light and with enough room for a person to squeeze through.

"We'll get rid of her just like we did Andrea," Gary was saying. "I'm building a shed for old man McMurtrey out on Old String Road. We'll put her under that cement. Nobody will know."

Zack whacked something with the palm of his hand. "You and your stupid ideas! When she turns up missing, don't you think Grant Hendley is going to suspect she might be buried like Andrea was? Don't you imagine he suspects you, my good friend, and will search through Ventris County for any new building that's going on? What happened to our plan for making Jasper Harris look like he's the murderer? If we plant some evidence at his place, it'll look like he killed Darcy and Andrea, too."

Gary sat silently for a few seconds and then muttered, "Don't get too big for your britches, Zack. You're in this as deep as I am. If you don't like my idea, you'd better come up with another one. We've got your cousin now and we can't let her go. She knows too much and she keeps poking into my business; says she's just writing a book. So we're going to have to get rid of her one way or another."

"And you are dead set on staying here and pretending to be innocent of any crime?" Zack asked. "Your greed is going to get you into trouble, Boss."

"Look, Zack, you are being well paid for driving my truck from California to Oklahoma. Nobody knows I'm bringing in drugs to the dealers around here. Everybody thinks you're just bringing in building materials. So I think when you say I'm greedy, it's a case of the pot calling the kettle black. You didn't have to be a part of this."

"And now that I am, I can't get out. I hadn't planned on murder, Gary. And if you'd been more careful, Andrea would never have caught on about the drugs."

"Oh, shut up. Point is, she did find out and she said she was going to turn me in, so what else could I do? Then when I threatened her, she promised she wouldn't tell but she said she wanted a divorce. Did you know that, Zack? If she had left, she would have taken all her wonderful money with her. And my wife was loaded with dough. I've gotta admit I've put it to good use."

"And I helped by letting you use my ATV to haul her away, didn't I? Seems to me like I'm the one doing all the helping and you're the one getting the 'wonderful money' as you called it."

"Point is, Zack, you did help and you are in this as deep as I am now."

Zack snorted. "I'm going to go for my four-wheeler so we can get Darcy out of here the back way, like we did Andrea," Zack said. "When I get back, we can decide what to do with my nosy cousin."

The two men left. The sound of their boots crunching through dry leaves grew fainter.

Gary and Zack were into drugs. A lucrative and deadly business. I had learned a lot about this type of criminal when I was an investigative reporter. Most drug dealers don't have to worry about old age. They have short lives. These two men could have found no more detestable way to make money.

A cold sweat broke out on my body. My stomach lurched and I swallowed hard to keep from throwing up. They planned to kill me. Gary had a small criminal empire going and they wouldn't let anybody stand in their way: not Gary's wife and certainly not me. My life had probably shortened considerably. I would live just until Zack came back with his ATV. I tried to pray and a snatch of Psalm 91 came to mind: "For He shall give His angels charge over you."

"Please, Lord, I need Your angels now," I whispered. Those ancient words gave me a measure of calm. My purse sat by the big front door. Gary and Zack had been lax in leaving it there but then again, why not? I was trussed up like a Thanksgiving turkey and they seemed pretty sure I'd still be in the same place waiting for them when they decided to return and end my life.

Well, end it they might, but I was determined not to cooperate. Sometimes panic sharpens the senses and mine were revved into high gear. I looked frantically around for a way out of my prison. A tall support beam reaching from the floor into the dark loft of the barn was a few feet away. I rolled over to it. Propping my back against the support, I pulled my feet under me and slowly pushed my way up.

My legs wobbled and threatened to crumple under me. I took a few deep breaths. Now what? True, for the moment my feet were holding me up but they were securely tied together. What should I do? Could I hop out the door and hop my way to freedom? But where would I hide? When Gary and Zack realized I was not in the barn, they would probably find me in no time. After all, I could not go very fast and they would have Zack's ATV. Gary probably knew every hiding place on his ranch. Could I reach my purse and had they left my gun inside? There was only one way to find out.

I pushed away from the beam and hopped toward my purse. Dropping down to my knees, I scooted around until I touched it as it lay behind me. I felt the clasp at the top, popped it open, and with the fingertips of both hands, began rummaging through. The gun and cell phone were gone.

Tears stung my eyes. Now what? Could I hide behind something in the barn and hope that Zack and Gary would not find me? As soon as the idea flashed into my mind, I realized I was grasping at straws. I would have a better chance out in the open. If I could make it to the thick woods, I just might be able to hide. With any luck, Gary was in the house and wouldn't look out his window to see me. How far was it to the Crowder home? I might have thirty minutes before Zack got back with his four-wheeler. How far could I hop in thirty minutes? Then again, Zack might be back in less time than that.

My heart beat so fast that breathing hurt. Why had I been so careless as to get caught? The answer came immediately: because I trusted Zack. When he said Gary would be out of town, I believed him. What a traitor!

My fingers touched a bulge within the zipped-up pocket inside my purse. It wasn't the gun nor the cell phone. I felt around its shape. It was a knife—Jackson Conner's knife. Zack and Gary either hadn't found it or hadn't thought it was important. After all, what could I do with my hands securely bound behind me? I was about to find out.

I had often heard someone say, "I could do that with my hands tied behind my back." I would be willing to bet they never tried unzipping a compartment inside a purse, fishing out a pocketknife, and trying to open the blade of said knife, simply by feeling, and all the while shaking like a leaf.

After dropping the knife into the bottom of my purse three times, I finally got a firm grip with my left hand. I could feel the indentation where two blades fit snugly inside the knife but which was the long blade and which was the short? I settled on one, slid a fingernail into the groove on the blade and tried to pry it open. It slipped out of my hands and fell. This time it missed the purse and clunked against the wood floor.

I blindly fished around until once again I had it in my fingers.

At last I held the knife with my right hand and popped open a blade. I slid the blade under the rope on my left wrist. I sawed back and forth, back and forth, praying that the knives Gary Worth had used as a promotional had good, sharp blades. At last the rope around my wrist snapped and dropped away.

My shoulders ached and the muscles in my arms felt as if they were going into a full-blown spasm, but my hands were free. I held them out in front of my face and wiggled my fingers. My left wrist had small, bloody cuts but that was okay. The important thing was, my hands were free. Using my left hand, I removed the rope dangling from my right wrist then set to work on the ropes binding my ankles.

When my feet were free, I felt like dancing; instead, I used one of the old kegs by the door as support and pulled myself up. Hopefully, the feeling would soon return to my legs and arms. Surely, since I had come this far in my fight for freedom, I could slip through that barn door and run toward the road and safety. I had my hand on the door and was about to squeeze through when I heard the sound of a small motor. The noise grew louder. It was unmistakably the roar of an ATV. The motor stopped and heavy footsteps swished through the fallen leaves toward the barn. Cousin Zack had returned.

CHAPTER 33

Where could I hide? Or should I look for a possible escape? A ladder nailed to the far wall reached into the dim recess of the hayloft. Would I have time to dash for the ladder and clamber up out of sight? My answer came when I heard Zack just outside the door.

"I hope Gary has made himself useful while I was gone," he muttered.

My leg bumped into something hard that was leaning against the sliding door. I looked down. A mallet—a heavy, wood maul was once an essential tool for every farmer. Thankfully, Gary had not seen fit to rid himself of this one. I picked it up and my arms sagged with the weight of it.

Zack stepped inside the barn and squinted toward the back where he had left me. "What the—" he began, but he didn't have time to finish his sentence.

Swinging the mallet up and over, I brought it down on the head of this despicable human being. He dropped like a rock and sprawled full length at the door of the barn.

He didn't move when I nudged him with my foot. "Oh, dear Lord, I hope to goodness I haven't killed him," I whispered. But I'd worry about that later. I didn't have time right now. Gary would be coming out soon. He and Zack had planned to decide what to do with me when Zack got back. I didn't want Gary to see Zack knocked out cold on the floor of the barn.

Would Gary see me if I made a run for it? Maybe that wouldn't be wise. What I had done to Zack I could also do to Gary as he came through the door but I was going to have to get Zack out of sight. Then maybe while Gary was bending over Zack, I could knock him out, too.

Somewhere in the back of my mind I realized I wasn't thinking clearly. How long would Zack stay unconscious? If Gary could see Zack's prostrate body before he got into the barn, he would be on guard.

I grabbed Zack's boot and tugged. He moved a couple of inches. I pulled again and Zack slid another two inches. Grunting and sweating, I moved him inch by slow inch. At last, the full length of Zack Crowder lay out of sight of anyone standing outside the open doorway.

Dropping Zack's foot, I ran back to get my mallet. At least with it, I wouldn't be defenseless. I planned for Gary to lie there beside his partner in crime very soon.

An arm reached through the door and grabbed me.

"Not so fast," Gary growled.

In my fervor of moving Zack and the scraping noise he had made across the floor, I hadn't heard Gary's approach. I mentally kicked myself for letting this happen a second time.

Adrenalin was pumping and I found a strength I didn't know I had. "Let go of me, you vermin! You worm!" I yelled. I twisted and turned but he pinned my arms down to my side.

Gary kicked my feet out from under me and I sat down abruptly. He stood over me, a pistol pointed directly at my head.

His face contorted into something that reminded me of a wild animal. "I should have done this in the first place," he snarled.

I rolled to one side and felt the breath of the bullet as it hissed past my face. Gary was leveling the gun for a second shot but that shot never came. Another explosion echoed throughout the barn and Gary dropped to the floor, his weapon flying off into the shadows.

Grant appeared in the doorway, his gun drawn. He looked down at Gary who was moaning and holding his leg. Jim Clendon came in behind Grant. He unhooked some handcuffs from his belt and knelt down beside the wounded Gary.

"I'm bleeding," Gary moaned. "I'm bleeding to death."

Clendon grinned at him. "Probably not. But then, you can't ever tell about these bullet wounds."

Grant sheathed his gun and walked toward me. "Darcy, did they hurt you? Are you all right?"

I ran into his arms and clung to him as I tried to stop shaking.

"Oh, Grant, I'm all right now. Thank God you came."

CHAPTER 34

"At least I know where Andrea is now," Sophie said. "I know that she is at peace. I am going to have her buried at home, at Inglenook."

"That's the right thing to do," I said. "Andrea would not want to be anywhere else."

"Do you need your cup filled, Grant?" Mom asked, bustling around the table with her old yellow coffee pot.

He put his hand over the top of his mug. "No, thanks, Miss Flora. I'm pretty well stocked up on my supply of caffeine for a week or three."

"I agree, Aunt Sophie. It's Andrea's ranch and, by the way, I had a talk with Tom last night, by telephone. I decided to take your advice. If he had been kinder to Andrea, who knows? She might still be alive. I don't want Tom Mott after all."

For the first time I noticed that Charlene's left hand was devoid of that big diamond.

Mom put the coffee pot on the table and sat down next to Jackson Conner.

"You know, Charlene, that ranch really should be yours by rights. It certainly makes sense. Jackson, do you think you could look at the legalities and see what we can do?" Sophie asked.

Jackson Conner nodded. "I'll be glad to look into it."

"What about Earlene, Mom? Have you talked to her since Zack was arrested?"

"I've tried but she won't speak to me. You know, she sat right by her son's bed all the time he was in the hospital and she wouldn't see anybody. Now that he's in jail, she keeps all the curtains drawn in her house. I guess she and J. Lee are grieving in their own way."

"I'm glad I didn't hit Zack hard enough to kill him."

I looked at these people sitting around my mother's table on this autumn morning and felt a warm rush of affection for each one. Two days had passed since I opened my eyes and found myself a prisoner in Gary Worth's barn. I shivered and lifted my coffee cup.

"Cold, Darcy?" Grant patted my shoulder.

"No, just thinking of some 'what ifs.' I'd like to propose a toast."

"Hear, hear," Jackson said.

"I want to thank all of you, my family and friends, for caring and for helping and for gathering here at Mom's table. You are special and dear to me. So I want to drink to all of you."

Mom lifted her cup. "I add my thanks to Darcy's."

Sophie wiped tears from her eyes. "Words can't express how grateful I am for your help, Darcy and Flora, and Grant. You didn't give up, even though your own lives were in danger. And I'm very thankful that we have all come through this ordeal together."

Cups lifted and clinked together over the table.

"Grant," I said, "if you hadn't come into the barn when you did, this wouldn't be happening now. Gary and Zack might still be scot-free instead of in the Ventris County jail. And I might be . . . might be . . . ."

"But you're not," Mom said. "And I don't know how to say thank you, Grant, for giving me back my daughter."

"How did you know where to find me?" I asked him.

Grant rubbed the side of his nose. "We had been keeping an eye on Gary for a while. We suspected he was bringing in drugs but we could never catch him. And, we suspected Zack Crowder knew more than he should about it. Jim Clendon was staked out at Zack's, watching his place. When Jim saw Zack take out his ATV, he phoned me and we followed him."

I smiled across the table at Jackson Conner. "I'm glad you left your pocketknife on the kitchen table, Mr. Conner. If you hadn't, well, I don't know . . . ."

"The point is, I did, Darcy. No use dwelling on all those 'what ifs.'"

Mom scooted the yellow coffee pot across the table. "Grant, I just know you need some more.

Grant shrugged, picked up the pot and poured a cupful.

"Grant, did you ever find out who it was at Spirit Leap that night? Or maybe it was my imagination."

"Never found a thing, Darcy. Sorry."

Sophie scooted back from the table. "Charlene and I need to go back to Amarillo. I've got to talk to some of Andrea's friends. They will want to come to her memorial service."

She was interrupted by a knock at the door. Mom looked at me questioningly.

"I'll go, Mom," I said. "Just sit still."

Jasper Harris stood on the front porch, twisting his ball cap round and round. "Miss Darcy, may I come in? I need to tell you all something."

"Well, sure. Of course, Jasper." Was he well? Jasper hid away from people. He wouldn't even come home if he saw a car in his own driveway. And now he was here, when he could plainly see there were three extra cars in front of my mother's house? I would have to circle this date on the calendar.

Everyone at the table looked up as Jasper followed me into the kitchen. His face grew red and he shifted his weight from one foot to the other.

Mom smiled at him. "Jasper, would you like some coffee? I have cookies on the counter. I'll bet you are hungry."

"No, thanks, Miss Flora," he mumbled. "Sheriff, I reckon it's just as well you're here, too, 'cause I got something to confess. I hope I ain't broke no laws but, well, I just gotta get it off my chest. I've been worrying about it."

Grant looked sharply at him. "Go ahead, Jasper."

I had wondered what Jasper knew about Andrea's burial. Maybe he was going to tell us that he saw who put her under Pat's garage floor.

Jasper cleared his throat and ran a finger under the collar of his blue-checked shirt. "There's actually a couple of things I gotta confess. I was out in the woods two years ago when Zack brought Andrea down that trail back of Worth's house. He was on his ATV and he had her in a little trailer thing behind him. It was dark and I didn't know it was Andrea, but after I heard she was missing, I . . . well, I just put two and two together."

Sophie made a choking sound and covered her face with her hands.

Grant frowned. "Jasper, you should have come to me right away. You know that, don't you?"

Jasper nodded. "Yes, sir."

Grant's chair scraped the floor as he pushed away from the table and stood up. "You may have to testify in court, Jasper. Don't you go running away anywhere, you understand? If you do, you'll be in trouble, too."

Jasper bit his lip and looked at the floor. "There's something else. You remember, Miss Darcy, when you were out at Spirit Leap? Fact is, I was there, too. I didn't think you saw me. I was back in the timber. You see, I'd been trailing a mountain lion. I saw one sneakin' around our house and I was afraid he was going to get poor ole Murphy, my hound dog. So I got my rifle and I started trailing him. He came right through your pasture, Miss Darcy."

I put up my hand. "Wait, wait a minute. Was that you that I heard back in the woods when I was sitting out at Spirit Leap?"

He nodded and dropped his head. "'Fraid so. But you weren't in danger from me. You were in danger from that big cat. I think he may have been watching you, Miss Darcy, and I scared him off when I came. I guess you heard him or me. You jumped up and ran like a jackrabbit to the house. I watched until I knew you were safe back at Miss Flora's."

"Jasper, do you have a knife?" I asked.

"Yep, one I got from Gary Worth quite a while back. He was givin' them out for free but I lost it somewhere around. Why? Did you find it?"

Grant nodded. "She found it by that big boulder she was sitting on. Did you happen to be over there?"

"I guess so. I walked around some after I saw Miss Darcy was safe from the mountain lion. I'm sure glad you found it. It's a good knife."

I put my arms around Jasper and gave him a hug. "You'll never know how happy I am that you told us this. Thanks, Jasper. You've been a good friend."

He stood stiffly enduring my hug and turned even redder.

"Stop by the office tomorrow, Jasper," Grant said. "I've got your knife and I'll be glad to give it back."

Jasper nodded and grinned. Then he bolted for the front door. We heard it slam behind him.

Mom sighed. "Well, I guess the last part of the mystery is solved now; all the loose ends tied up."

Sophie pushed back her chair. She and Charlene stood up. "For some reason, I feel stronger than I've felt in a long time," she said. "Maybe it's just because this horrible nightmare is over."

Nightmares. Hopefully, they would quit plaguing my dreams one of these nights. After hugs and handshakes, Sophie and Charlene went out the door and climbed into Charlene's little sports car.

"Mom, when you got that letter from Sophie we had no idea what reading it would get us into. But I'm grateful that Sophie knows now that her daughter is at peace."

The phone rang. Not good timing on the part of the caller, but I excused myself and hurried to answer it.

"Got that info for you, Darcy." Max Sutton was always direct and didn't mince words.

"I'd know your voice anywhere, Maxie. What did you find out?"

"Gary's dad, the senior Worth, was in the residential construction business for many years and evidently did good work and had a solid business reputation. Then the old man got sick and Gary took over. He changed the name of the business to Cobblestone Homes and changed everything else about it too—used cheap materials, did shoddy work, and soon became blacklisted in the construction business. His dad died right before Gary did all that. I guess Gary inherited his dad's money."

"How long ago was that, Maxie?"

"Probably seven or eight years. Everybody expected him to go through his wad and go bust but suddenly, although he was putting up fewer and fewer buildings, his financial situation looked like it improved. There were speculations as to why this happened. Then rumors began to circulate about Gary and drugs. Just rumors, mind you. Nothing he could be arrested for."

"Thanks, Maxie. I believe you are right. Gary was heavily involved in drug traffic. But right now he's in jail and we've found his wife. He killed her, Maxie, to keep her quiet."

There was silence on the Texas end of the phone call. Then I heard Maxie draw a deep breath. "Well, keep me posted," he said. "I'd love to break that story."

And on that note I replaced the phone and rejoined Mom, Jackson, and Grant.

"An important call?" Mom asked.

I smiled. "Yes, Maxie called from Dallas, filling in some blanks about Gary Worth."

Grant groaned. "That is one name I'll be glad not to hear again. I'm finishing up some paper work and then he'll be the problem of the federal boys, I hope."

"I don't want to think about him again either, Grant," I said.

In fact, I didn't want to think about anything more important than starting on that book Amy suggested or whether the coffee pot was full. I would banish any thoughts of being involved in another missing person drama or murder or mayhem in any form, at least not for a long, long time.

Then Mom brought up another prospect. "We'll need to get started on that new house as soon as possible. It'll be the prettiest house in Ventris County and have enough bedrooms for everybody close to us."

Wow! I thought she'd back out of her new house plans as soon as we distanced ourselves from that emotional scene on Granny Grace's land.

"In fact," she continued, "I've already been looking at building plans and talking with a couple of construction companies. With a little luck, we should be able to move in by spring." The look she gave Grant was sly. "Then we'll put up a big sign with black and gold borders that says *Tucker and Campbell, Private Investigators.*"

That astonished me. My poor, brave, mother had been through so much lately, yet she managed to keep her sense of humor. I grinned, thinking about what Jake had once said about her: "Your mom is one tough old gal!"

Grant slapped the table with both hands. "Oh, no, please don't put out any sign Miss Flora. I don't think I can stand any more of the worry and sleepless nights I went through wondering if the two of you were going to get yourselves killed while you were trying to do things law enforcement should have been handling."

"Besides," he pushed his chair back, "I've got another job in mind for Darcy."

He got up, came around the table and reached for my hand. He didn't need to elaborate on what job he had in mind. His warm blue eyes said it all.

I rose and went into his arms.

— THE END —

It may seem strange to some that a mild-mannered kindergarten teacher would become an author of cozy mysteries, but it's actually a good fit. A teacher is a word craft. So is a writer. A teacher wants the efforts of her labor to have a positive outcome. So does a writer. A teacher prays and hopes that each student has a positive take-away from her work. A writer hopes that for her readers too. A teacher would like each of the children in her classroom to achieve a satisfying life. Although she can't control that, as a writer she can control the way her books conclude!

A native Oklahoman, Blanche has a deep familiarity with the Sooner state, so it's the logical setting for her books. Her Cherokee heritage and feeling at home in the rural settings of Oklahoma are vividly woven into the background fabric of her books. Her other published cozies include *The Cemetery Club* and *Best Left Buried*, books one and three on the Flora/Darcy Series, co-authored by Barbara Burgess.

Barbara Burgess is a retired trial court administrator who says she found many good story ideas in the courtroom. One of those ideas evolved into her first suspense novel, *Lethal Justice*, published in 2010. She also co-authored *The Cemetery Club*, a mystery novel based on Cherokee history. Her father was half Cherokee and she says much of her family history involves Cherokee legend and beliefs similar to those found in *Grave Shift*. She has also written short fiction for *Woman's World* and Alfred Hitchcock's *Mystery Magazine* and freelanced for several Arkansas newspapers.